The Spotted Leopard raised the
bunny high in the air

See page 150.

Uncle Wiggily's Picture Book

by Howard R. Garis

Illustrated by Lansing Campbell

PLATT & MUNK, PUBLISHERS · *New York*
A division of Grosset & Dunlap

Look For These Other UNCLE WIGGILY Books:

UNCLE WIGGILY AND HIS FRIENDS
UNCLE WIGGILY'S STORY BOOK
UNCLE WIGGILY TO THE RESCUE
(also available on audio cassette)

UNCLE WIGGILY'S WELCOME

DEAR CHILDREN:

Opening the covers of a book is like opening the front door of a house, so that you may go inside and have jolly times. And how good it is when some one who loves you stands at the front door and says:

"Oh, how glad I am to see you!"

That is what I say to you now, as you open this book.

"Come in and have some jolly fun with me!"

You know that I love you, children, and I want you to enjoy these stories about me. They tell how I escaped from the bad chaps who wanted to catch me. The pictures show what tricks I played on the Fuzzy Fox, the Woozie Wolf and the Puffing Pipsisewah so they might not nibble my ears. Then, also, there are tales of some of the animal children whom you well know.

So then, having opened the covers of this book, come in and read! Stay as long as you wish, and, when you go out, invite some one else to enter.

Your loving friend,

UNCLE WIGGILY.

CONTENTS

Uncle Wiggily's Picture Book

STORY I

UNCLE WIGGILY AND SAMMIE LITTLETAIL

ONCE upon a time, not so very many years ago, Uncle Wiggily Longears, a rabbit gentleman who lived in a hollow stump bungalow, started out to look for an adventure.

"What sort of adventure do you think will happen to you today?" asked Nurse Jane Fuzzy Wuzzy, the muskrat lady housekeeper with whom Uncle Wiggily lived.

"That I don't know," answered the bunny. "So many strange and queer things happen that I never can tell what they are going to be. One thing I hope, however—I don't want to meet the Pipsisewah or Skeezicks when I am hopping around to-day!"

"Gracious me sakes alive and a basket of soap bubbles!" cried Nurse Jane. "I should say no indeed! But where are you going, Uncle Wiggily?"

"Oh, just to hop over the fields and through the woods," answered Mr. Longears. "Is there anything I may have the

3

pleasure of doing for you, Nurse Jane?" inquired the bunny, with a low and polite bow.

"Yes, I did want something from the store," replied Miss Fuzzy Wuzzy. "And for fear you may forget it I have written the name of it down on this sugar cookie." She showed Uncle Wiggily a white cookie with something written on it in pink candy-letters.

"Ha! Ha! What is the idea of this?" asked the bunny, as he put the sugar cookie in his pocket.

"So you will remember to get me what I want," answered Nurse Jane with a smile that made the hair ribbon on her tail jiggle like a jumping-jack. "When you get hungry, as I'm sure you will, then you will eat the sugar cookie I have given you. And when you eat it you will read what I have written on it in pink candy-letters. Then you will remember and go to the store to get it."

"Ha! That's a very good idea!" laughed Uncle Wiggily, as he looked in his pocket to make sure he had not lost the cookie. "I'll be sure to remember, Nurse Jane. Good-bye for a while!"

Away he hopped, over the fields and through the woods, and, all of a sudden, the bunny gentleman heard a rustling in the bushes.

"Oh, ho! Just my luck!" whispered Mr. Longears to himself. "I suppose this is the Woozie Wolf or the Bad Bob Cat!"

The bunny gentleman crouched down under a little, next-year's Christmas tree, and he was trying to bend his ears sideways so they would not show so plainly, when suddenly a little rabbit boy hopped out from beneath a bush, and stood looking around curious-like.

"Why, Sammie Littletail!" cried Uncle Wiggily, when he saw who it was. "What are you doing here?"

"I'm looking for a mud puddle," answered Sammie.

"A mud puddle!" exclaimed the gentleman rabbit in great surprise. "Why in the world are you looking for a mud puddle? Most boys, or girls too, for that matter, want to keep as far away from mud puddles as they can! And here you are looking for one! Dear me, Sammie Littletail, I hope——"

"Excuse me for interrupting you, Uncle Wiggily," spoke Sammie politely, trying to make his little pink nose twinkle as did his uncle's larger one; "excuse me, but the reason I am looking for a mud puddle is so that I may try my new boots."

"Your new boots?" asked Uncle Wiggily, wondering still more.

"Yes," replied Sammie, as he stuck out his little hind legs. "Daddy just bought me these new rubber boots, and I want to find a mud puddle so I can wade in and see if they leak. I was hoping it would rain, so I could go out and splash around, but it doesn't seem to be going to shower," and Sammie looked somewhat sadly up at the bright blue sky and shining sun.

"It is a lovely day," said Mr. Longears. "No rain in sight."

"Then please help me find a mud puddle," begged the bunny boy.

"I will!" laughed Uncle Wiggily. "And I hope your boots don't leak, Sammie."

"Oh, they oughtn't to leak, being new," Sammie exclaimed.

But something worse was going to happen him. Read on, if you please, a little bit farther!

"Come along, Sammie," called Uncle Wiggily, after gnawing from a tree a bit of sweet birch bark, and giving some to the rabbit boy. "We'll hop this way and that way to look for a big mud puddle."

On together hopped Uncle Wiggily and Sammie, and in a short time they reached a meadow in which Mrs. Moo Cow was eating grass.

"Any mud puddles over there?" called Uncle Wiggily, politely.

"Moo! Moo!" answered the cow lady. "Moo!"

"She says there are two!" cried Sammie. "Hurry up so I can try my new boots!"

"She didn't say 'two'—she said 'moo!' which is her way of wishing us good-day, Sammie," spoke Uncle Wiggily. "But perhaps there may be just one mud puddle there. We'll take a look!"

Over into the meadow hopped Uncle Wiggily and Sammie, and, surely enough, there was just the nicest mud puddle for which heart could wish! It was all squidgie-squodgie, mucky mud, with a pool of water in the centre.

"Oh this will be a dandy place to try my boots!" cried Sammie. "I'm going to wade in, Uncle Wiggily."

"All right, but don't go too far!" advised the bunny rabbit gentleman. And then, as he watched Sammie wading out from shore, Uncle Wiggily happened to put his paw in his pocket and he found the sugar cookie that Nurse Jane had given him.

"This reminds me that I am hungry," said the bunny uncle to himself. "I'll eat this cookie and give Sammie a bit when he comes out after trying his new boots in the mud puddle."

But as Uncle Wiggily began to eat the sugar cookie he saw the pink candy letters on it.

"Oh, ho! This makes me think of something else," said Mr. Longears, as he read the words Miss Fuzzy Wuzzy had written. "I must go to the store and get what Nurse Jane wants. I say there, Sammie!" called Uncle Wiggily.

"Yes, what is it?" Sammie inquired. "Oh, you ought to see my boots, Uncle Wiggily!" cried the rabbit boy. "They're all covered with mud, and they don't leak a bit!"

"That's good," answered the rabbit uncle. "But listen, Sammie, as the telephone girl says. I have to go to the store to get something for Nurse Jane. Wait here for me until I come back."

"All right," answered Sammie. "I will. I'm having fun!"

Away hopped Uncle Wiggily. He reached the store, bought what Nurse Jane had written down on the sugar cookie for him to get, and with it he hopped back to the meadow.

"Hurry, Uncle Wiggily! Hurry!" cried Mrs. Moo Cow, as the bunny was skipping along the road. "Hurry and help Sammie!"

"What's the matter with Sammie?" asked Mr. Longears, his pink nose beginning to twinkle sideways because he was so excited.

"Oh, he's stuck in the mud puddle with his new boots, and he can't get out!" mooed Mrs. Cow.

Uncle Wiggily quickly hopped over the fence and, surely

enough, there was poor Sammie, away out in the middle of the puddle of mud.

"Come here!" cried Uncle Wiggily. "Come here right away!"

"My boots are stuck in the sticky mud!"

"I—I can't!" sobbed Sammie. "My boots are stuck in the sticky mud!"

"Well, jump out of your boots and wade over here in your stocking feet!" said Uncle Wiggily.

"No! No, indeed!" cried Sammie. "Do you think I'm going to leave my new boots stuck in the mud? I won't come out unless they do!"

"Dear me! What trouble!" cried Uncle Wiggily. "What am I to do?"

"Get a long rail from the fence, Uncle Wiggily," advised Mrs. Moo Cow. "You stand on the edge of the puddle, and hold the rail out to Sammie. He can catch hold of it in his paws, and you can pull him out of the sticky mud; rabbit boy, boots and all."

"Thank you! I'll try that," said the bunny.

As he was getting a rail from the fence Uncle Wiggily suddenly heard a queer noise near a big rock.

"Oh, I hope that is no bad animal getting ready to jump out at me!" thought the bunny gentleman. "I must hurry and save Sammie and then hop home with him! I hope no bad animal gets me!"

Uncle Wiggily held out the fence rail across the mud puddle. Sammie grasped it in his front paws. There was a long pull, and a strong pull. There was a squidgie-squodgie sound as his boots and the rabbit boy in them were pulled up out of the sticky-ickie mud, and then Uncle Wiggily hauled Sammie safely to the solid bank of the puddle.

"My, Sammie! You were in great danger!" said Uncle Wiggily. "I am glad I pulled you out, but you were in great danger!"

"Yes, maybe I was!" agreed the rabbit boy, as he ate a little piece of the sugar cookie Mr. Longears had saved for him. "But, anyhow, my boots didn't leak, and I guess—Oh,

Uncle Wiggily! Oh, look what's coming! Look! Look!" quickly cried Sammie.

And then,
             ALL
                  OF
                       A
                            SUDDEN
out from behind a big rock came a bad Bob Cat and caught Uncle Wiggily, howling "I want ears!"

"Excuse me!" said Uncle Wiggily. "Your claws need cutting!" And taking from his pocket the long pair of scissors which he had bought for Nurse Jane, he began to cut the bad Bob Cat's claws.

The bad Bob Cat was so scared at this, that he ran away.

Thus Uncle Wiggily drove away the bad animal that tried to nibble his ears, and everything came out all right, for which I am very thankful, and I hope you are the same.

Then the bunny gentleman helped Sammie wash the mud off his new boots, the rabbit boy ate the piece of sugar cookie his uncle had saved for him, and as he picked up the last crumbs he said:

"Do you know what that tastes like, Uncle Wiggily?"

"No, perhaps I don't exactly know, Sammie boy. What does that piece of sugar cookie taste like?"

"More!" answered the bunny chap with a laugh. "It tastes just like more!"

"Then we had better hop back to the bungalow and get some more!" chuckled Mr. Longears.

So away they hopped, and if the apple dumpling doesn't try to turn into a peach shortcake, when the gold fish wants to ride on its back, I'll tell you next about Uncle Wiggily and Susie Littletail.

STORY II

UNCLE WIGGILY AND SUSIE LITTLETAIL

"WAIT a moment, Uncle Wiggily! Please wait a moment!" called Nurse Jane Fuzzy Wuzzy, one morning, as the bunny rabbit gentleman was hopping away from his hollow stump bungalow. "Why are you in such a hurry?"

"Well, I'm not in any special hurry," answered Mr. Longears, as he stopped to see if the rain water barrel needed a drink; but it didn't. "I'm just going to look for an adventure," went on the bunny uncle. "Do you want to come with me?"

"Dear me! I should say not!" laughed the muskrat lady housekeeper as she brushed a wisp of cobweb off her whiskers. "I am too busy to go adventuring to-day. But the reason I asked you to wait a moment is because I want you to get me something from the store."

"Right gladly will I do that!" spoke Uncle Wiggily, with a low polite bow, such as he always made when Nurse Jane asked him to do her a favor. "What is it you wish me to bring? Are you going to write it down on a sugar cookie, as you did before?"

"You mean the time you pulled Sammie Littletail and his new boots out of the mud puddle?" inquired Nurse Jane.

"Yes; that's the time," answered the bunny.

"No, I'm not going to give you a sugar cookie now," said the muskrat lady with a happy smile. "I will tie this piece

12

of red yarn around your paw, and, when it tickles you, then you'll remember what you are to bring me."

"But what am I to bring you?" asked the bunny gentleman as Miss Fuzzy Wuzzy tied on the bit of soft yarn.

"Oh, that's so—I was nearly forgetting to tell you what I wanted!" laughed the muskrat lady. "Well, I'll whisper it to you, and perhaps that will make you remember it better."

So she whispered in the bunny's ear, and Uncle Wiggily suddenly cried:

"Stop! Don't do that again!"

"What's the matter?" Nurse Jane asked.

"You tickle me when you whisper!" chuckled Mr. Longears. "Goodness how you tickled!"

"All the better for making you remember," remarked Miss Fuzzy Wuzzy, and then Uncle Wiggily hopped over the fields and through the woods.

"I have two things to do this day," said the bunny to himself as he stopped to smell a red flower growing in the green grass. "I must go to the store for Nurse Jane, and I must find an adventure.

"Let me see now," went on the bunny thoughtfully. "Which shall I do first?"

"I wish you would do something for me, first!" suddenly spoke a voice, seeming to come from behind a big stump.

"Goodness me! Who's that?" gasped Uncle Wiggily. "Not the Bad Bob Cat or a Wild Boar, I hope!"

"No, indeed!" laughed a voice in a most jolly fashion. "I'm a friend of yours, Uncle Wiggily!" And out from behind the stump came Susie Littletail, the rabbit girl.

"Oh, Susie! I'm so glad to see you!" cried Uncle Wiggily.

"And I'm glad to see you!" said the little rabbit girl. "Did you think I was one of the bad animals?"

"I thought you were the Heavy Hippopotamus at the very least!" exclaimed Uncle Wiggily, laughing again. "But what is it you want me to do for you, Susie?"

"Oh, I want you to help me make a hammock for my new doll, Marion Matilda Orange Pie," said Susie.

"Marion Matilda Orange Pie!" gasped Uncle Wiggily. "What a strange name for a doll!"

"Well, she is a very strange doll!" remarked Susie. "She never will go to sleep unless she is lying in a hammock. I took her out for a walk, but I forgot and left her hammock home. Now she is so sleepy as never was, but she will not close her eyes unless I can put her in a hammock. Look!"

Susie held out her doll. Surely enough the eyes of Marion Matilda Orange Pie were wide, wide open!

"Unless I can put her in a hammock she will not go to sleep," went on Susie, "and she'll be as cross as two sticks and part of another. Oh, what am I going to do?"

"A hammock; eh?" questioned Uncle Wiggily. "But how am I to make a hammock out here? I have no rope or string or——"

"You can make a hammock, like a cat's cradle, out of some pieces of wild grape vine," explained Susie. "You did it once when you took me on a picnic. Please, Uncle Wiggily, make Marion Matilda Orange Pie a hammock out of a wild grape vine—but not too wild!" the rabbit girl hastened to say.

"Not too wild what?" asked Uncle Wiggily.

"Don't have the grape vine too wild," begged the little bunny girl. "If the vine is too wild it will keep jumping about all the while, and Marion will never get to sleep."

"That's so," said the gentleman bunny. "I'll take a piece of half-wild grape vine for the hammock, Susie."

This Uncle Wiggily did, gnawing down some trailing vine in the woods not far away. And from the vine he wove a sort of cat's cradle hammock for Susie's doll, hanging the hammock between two stumps.

"There, now your dollie can lie down, close her eyes and go to sleep," said the bunny gentleman, when the hammock was finished.

And, as truly as I'm telling you, no sooner had Susie placed Marion Matilda Orange Pie in the partly-wild grape vine hammock, than the doll closed her eyes and went fast, fast to sleep.

"Sush! Don't make any noise!" whispered Susie to Uncle Wiggily, holding her little paw up to her lips. "I don't want to have her wake up, or she may be as cross as three sticks."

"Yes, that's so!" whispered the bunny gentleman. "Well, I'll leave you here to watch your doll, Susie."

"Why, where are you going?" Susie wanted to know. "Can't you stay and play with me?"

Uncle Wiggily held out one paw with the piece of red yarn tied around it.

"This is to remind me of something Nurse Jane asked me to bring from the store for her," explained the bunny gentleman. "You swing Marion-whatever-her-name-is in the hammock until I come back, Susie."

"Yes, Uncle Wiggily, and thank you for being so kind," whispered Susie politely. "I'll wait here for you. It is so lovely and quiet in these weeds that I feel sleepy myself."

Susie was just going to close her eyes, and have a little sleep, when, all of a sudden, there was a rustling in the bushes, and the little rabbit girl sat up, wide awake in an instant.

"Who is there?" she cried. "Who are you and what do you want?"

Susie looked all around but could see no one. Then she heard the rustling sound again, and a gentle voice said:

"Dear little rabbit girl, could you please give a poor old tramp angle worm something to eat?" and over the path crawled the worm.

Susie was not afraid of worms, even tramp ones, so she looked kindly at the crawling creature and said:

"Of course I can give you something to eat. Here is a bit of carrot shortcake my doll didn't want."

"Oh, thank you!" murmured the tramp angle worm, and, taking the piece of cake, away he crawled.

"Now I'll go to sleep," said Susie.

Uncle Wiggily hopped along to the store, bought what Nurse Jane had told him to get for her, and as he hopped back toward the little mossy-green dingly-dell where he had left Susie, he heard the rabbit girl shouting loudly:

"Help! Help! Oh, Uncle Wiggily come and help me!"

"Goodness gracious sakes alive and a keyhole full of lollypops!" cried the bunny gentleman, hopping his very fastest. "Susie is in trouble! I hope no Lion, Tiger or Buffalo is chasing her!"

But when he reached the place where he had left Susie, and her doll in the hammock, Uncle Wiggily saw no bad

Susie was all tangled up in the grape vine hammock

animals. What he did see, however, made him give a big jump toward the two stumps.

For there, between them, was Susie all tangled up in the grape vine hammock with her doll; and Marion Matilda Orange Pie's eyes were wide open! Think of that!

"Oh, Susie! What happened?" cried Uncle Wiggily.

"Did the grape vine suddenly get wilder, and try to bite you?"

"Oh, no, nothing like that!" sobbed Susie. "But I was so tired and sleepy that I got into the hammock with Marion. I guess I was too heavy, for, all of a sudden, it broke down with me and I'm so tangled in the grape vine that I can't get out. Please help me!"

"Don't cry, Susie! I'll help you," said Uncle Wiggily kindly. "Wait a moment and I'll untangle you and Marion."

The bunny laid aside what he had bought for Nurse Jane, and reaching in amid the tangle of vine he began trying to help Susie.

"Come on! I have you!" cried the bunny, pulling on a leg. "Come on out!"

"Stop! Oh please stop!" begged Susie. "That's Marion's leg you're pulling on! If it comes off all the sawdust will run out, and she'll have to go to the hospital. Pull on my leg!"

"Oh, I thought that was your leg I had hold of!" said Uncle Wiggily. "Wait a moment now!"

By hard work; pulling here, pushing there, gnawing through the wild tangle of grape vine and untwisting it Uncle Wiggily at last got Susie free. Then he took out Marion Matilda Orange Pie, who, though she was wide awake, had not been hurt by the breaking hammock. Nor had Susie.

"My gracious sakes alive and an ice cream cone full of lolly-pops!" exclaimed Uncle Wiggily, as he sat down to rest, after the hard work of pulling Susie and her doll out of the tangled hammock. "That was quite an adventure, Susie! It was more of an adventure than any I have had to-day. For, to tell you the truth, nothing like an adventure has come my way yet."

"Oh, the day is early—cheer up!" laughed Susie, and Uncle Wiggily cheered up.

"Did anything else happen to you while I was gone?" asked the bunny gentleman.

"Yes," answered Susie, "I was almost asleep and a tramp ____"

"Don't tell me a tramp has been here!" cried Mr. Longears.

"Oh, it was just a tramp angle worm," laughed the little rabbit girl.

"Hark!" suddenly exclaimed Susie. "What's that noise?" She and Uncle Wiggily listened, bending their long, sharp ears down toward the earth. There was a rustling in the dried leaves and then a tiny little voice asked:

"Do you mind if I pick up some of these crumbs?"

"What crumbs?" inquired Uncle Wiggily, and then he and Susie saw a dear little old red ant lady mincing her way along over the dried leaves.

"Why, these crumbs here on the ground," replied the ant lady.

"I must have dropped some crumbs from the carrot short-cake when I gave it to the tramp angle worm," explained Susie. "Yes, dear ant lady, take all the crumbs you can find."

So she picked up the crumbs, Uncle Wiggily kindly pointing out some under a leaf that she might have missed, and then the bunny gentleman asked:

"Shall we hop along now, Susie?"

"Well, I guess Marion has had enough sleep," said Susie, "for she isn't a bit cross now. So let's go home, Uncle Wiggily."

But just as the bunny gentleman picked up what he had bought for Nurse Jane, there sounded a rustling noise in the bushes.

Susie screamed as she held her doll closer to her, and then the little rabbit girl cried:

"Oh, see what's coming, Uncle Wiggily! Look and see what's coming!"

And then ALL OF A SUDDEN, a roaring lion leaped out of the woods after the rabbit gentleman. But quick as a wink Uncle Wiggily picked up the broken grape vine hammock and threw it at the roaring lion who got all tangled up in it.

———

Away ran the bad animal, for he had had quite enough of trying to catch Uncle Wiggily, this time at least.

"Oh, how frightened I was!" sighed Susie, when it was all over. "Oh, so frightened!"

"No need to have been—no need at all!" laughed Uncle Wiggily. "I fixed that unpleasant chap all right! Is Marion Matilda Orange Pie feeling better?"

"Sush! Yes! She's gone to sleep again," whispered Susie. "I guess falling out of a hammock did her good!"

And perhaps it did; who knows?

So the bunny gentleman hopped safely home with Susie and her doll. And if the tea kettle sings a funny little song so the gas stove can do a dance on the kitchen oilcloth, I'll tell you next about Uncle Wiggily and Johnnie's kite.

STORY III

UNCLE WIGGILY AND JOHNNIE'S KITE

"UNCLE WIGGILY, have you some pieces of string you don't want?" inquired a voice outside an open window of the bunny rabbit's hollow stump bungalow one morning.

"What's that? A piece of string! Is the Gorilla or the Spotted Leopard trying to tie me up, to carry me off to their den so they can nibble my ears?" quickly asked Uncle Wiggily, tossing aside the cabbage leaf newspaper he had been reading, and looking down over the window sill.

"Oh, no, if you please! I'm neither Gorilla, Leopard nor yet the Bushy Bear!" laughed a jolly voice. Looking a little farther out, Uncle Wiggily saw Johnnie Bushytail, the squirrel boy.

"Oh, so it's you who wants the piece of string; is it?" asked Mr. Longears, trying to stop his pink nose from twinkling so fast, as it always did when he was a bit frightened.

"Yes, Uncle Wiggily, I'd like some string, if you have it," chattered Johnnie.

"Well, I guess I can find you some," kindly offered the bunny gentleman. Then getting up rather slowly, for his rheumatism was paining him that day, Uncle Wiggily found a ball of cord for the squirrel boy and handed it out through the window.

"Oh, thank you!" cried Johnnie, scampering away.

There was quiet for a few minutes, Uncle Wiggily was once

more peacefully reading his paper, looking to see if the price of carrots was any cheaper when, all of a sudden, a voice asked:

"Have you some thin sticks you don't want, Uncle Wiggily?"

"Thin sticks!" exclaimed the bunny, wadding his paper up into a big ball in his excitement. "Is that the Skeezicks who wants to beat me with sticks? Oh dear!"

"No, it is I—Johnnie the squirrel," was the answer. "I didn't mean to scare you, Uncle Wiggily!"

"Hum! Johnnie again!" grunted the bunny. "Maybe you didn't mean to scare me, but you did! And what is it you want now?"

"Sticks, if you please," chattered the squirrel chap.

"Oh—sticks—well, I'll see if I can find you any in the wood box," and, even though his rheumatism pained him, Uncle Wiggily limped out to the kitchen and through the open window handed Johnnie the thin sticks he had asked for.

"I do hope he'll leave you in peace and quiet now, Wiggy!" spoke Nurse Jane, the muskrat lady housekeeper.

"Oh, well, boys must play!" chuckled Mr. Longears, as he once more sat down to read the news from his crumpled paper.

But he had not turned more than two pages, and he was just looking at a funny picture of a cow lady having her horns polished, when, all of a quickness, a voice called through the window:

"Are you through with that paper, Uncle Wiggily? If you are would you mind letting me take it?"

"Eh? What's that? You want my paper? Are you the Skillery Scallery Alligator, and are you going to wrap me up in my paper and carry me away?" cried the bunny.

"No! No!" laughed a voice. "This is Johnnie Bushy-tail!"

"What—again?" cried the rabbit gentleman, and his heart did not beat so fast, nor did his pink nose twinkle so much, when he saw it was only his little squirrel friend. "Well, you may have the paper," went on the bunny gentleman. "There is no use trying to read when you are around!"

"Oh, thank you!" chattered Johnnie as his uncle tossed the paper out of the window.

"Say, Uncle Wiggily, don't you think you had better go and see what that squirrel boy is making with the string, sticks and paper?" advised Miss Fuzzy Wuzzy, as Johnnie scampered away. "He may be in some mischief!"

"Oh, Johnnie is a good squirrel," chuckled Uncle Wiggily. "But as I have nothing special to do I will take a little walk and see what is going on."

Johnnie was playing in the rabbit's bungalow yard, and, going down to the end of it, the bunny Uncle looked over the tall weeds to find out what was happening. He saw Johnnie with the string, paper and sticks all scattered around him.

"What are you making, Johnnie?" asked Uncle Wiggily.

"Oh, just a kite!" answered the squirrel boy. "And I'm so glad you came out, for I have nearly finished and I want you to help me fly it."

"A kite; eh?" exclaimed Mr. Longears. "I used to be

pretty good at making kites myself. Has this one a tail, Johnnie?"

"Yes, I had to make one with a tail, 'cause I don't know how to make the other kind yet," the squirrel boy said. "That's the reason I want you to help me fly it, Uncle Wiggily. I want you to hold the kite and tail up off the ground while I run with the string."

"Oh, I'll do that!" kindly offered the bunny. "I like to fly kites."

Soon Johnnie had tied the thin sticks together, he had strung some cord around their ends and over the sticks and string he had pasted the paper Uncle Wiggily gave him. Then he tied a long cord to his kite, fastened on the tail and it was ready to fly.

"Let's go out in front, where there aren't so many weeds for the tail to catch on," suggested Uncle Wiggily.

"All right," agreed Johnnie.

Uncle Wiggily was carrying the kite and its long tail, while the squirrel boy followed with the ball of cord, when Nurse Jane, looking from the window of the kitchen, where she was baking a lollypop pie, saw the bunny gentleman.

"Wiggy!" squealed the muskrat lady, rather excited like. "You don't mean to tell me you're going to fly a kite—at your age and with rheumatism so you can hardly walk! You aren't going to fly a kite; are you?"

"Oh, no, I'm not going to fly a kite — the *wind* will do that!" chuckled the bunny.

"Oh, ho! You feel like joking this morning, I see!" sniffed Miss Fuzzy Wuzzy sort of sarcastic like and with some disproportionability. "I thought your rheumatism pained you so you couldn't go over to Mrs. Twistytail's house for me and bring back what she borrowed yesterday."

"Oh, that's so—you did want me to get something for you from the pig lady," said Uncle Wiggily slowly. "I forgot about that. But, anyhow, my rheumatism is better, and I think if I help Johnnie fly his kite all the pain will stop, and then I can go to Mrs. Twistytail's for you."

"Let us hope so!" said Nurse Jane, patiently and resigned.

"Besides, all I am going to do is to hold the kite for him," went on the bunny. "Johnnie himself is going to run with it until the wind flies it."

"All right," spoke Miss Fuzzy Wuzzy. "You'll do as you please anyhow. Only don't forget to go to Mrs. Twisty-tail's."

"I'll remember," promised the bunny. "Come on now, Johnnie!" he whispered. "Let's fly the kite before she wants me to go somewhere else."

Uncle Wiggily and the squirrel boy went out in front of the bungalow. Johnnie unwound some of the cord and scampered down the road. Uncle Wiggily held the kite and its tail high in the air.

"All ready! Let go!" chattered Johnnie, and away he ran.

The kite went up in the air a little way and then it swooped down. And the worst of it was that just then Aunt Lettie, the goat lady, was passing along, and the tail of the kite tangled itself in her new hat that she had just bought at the fifteen and sixteen cent store.

"I'll grind you all up!" cried
the bunny.
"Oh, wow! Please don't! I'll be
good!" howled the hyena.

See page 30.

"Oh, dear me! Oh, my goodness!" bleated Aunt Lettie. "Oh! Oh!" She jumped up and down.

"Run, Johnnie! Run!" cried Uncle Wiggily, not seeing what had happened.

Away ran the squirrel boy, pulling on the string of his kite, and the tail was so twisted around Aunt Lettie's bonnet that it lifted the new hat right off the goat lady's head!

"Oh, stop! Stop! Your kite has my bonnet!"

"Oh, stop! Stop! Your kite has my bonnet!" bleated Aunt Lettie.

"Oh, dear me! Here's trouble!" sighed Uncle Wiggily.

Higher and higher soared the kite as Johnnie ran with it, taking Aunt Lettie's bonnet almost up to the clouds. The goat lady turned to the gentleman bunny, who was jumping up and down because he was so excited at seeing the kite fly, and Aunt Lettie said:

"I should think you'd be surprised at yourself, Uncle Wiggily, I really should; grabbing ladies' bonnets off like this! The very idea!"

"Oh, dear me!" cried the rabbit gentleman. "I didn't know this was going to happen!"

"Yes, and something worse is going to happen!" suddenly growled a whispering voice in the deep weeds at the side of the road.

But neither Uncle Wiggily nor Aunt Lettie heard this.

"Call Johnnie to stop running away with my bonnet!" begged Aunt Lettie, and the bunny did so.

"Oh, I didn't know your new hat was on my kite's tail!" laughed the squirrel boy, as he stopped running. "I'm so sorry!"

"Hum!" sniffed Aunt Lettie. "Uncle Wiggily is more to blame than you, Johnnie! He should know better at his age!"

"Oh, this is worse and worse!" sighed the poor rabbit uncle. "I must go!" he suddenly said. "Please excuse me! I promised to get something from Mrs. Twistytail for Nurse Jane. I'll be back in a moment. Excuse me!"

Away ran Uncle Wiggily, while Johnnie untangled his kite tail from Aunt Lettie's bonnet. It wasn't much damaged— I mean the kite's tail wasn't.

Aunt Lettie sat down on a smooth, round stone beside the path, and began to breathe very hard.

"Is—is anything the matter?" asked Johnnie, rather worried, for he had once seen his mother act this way when the chimney caught fire. "Is anything the matter, Aunt Lettie?" anxiously asked the squirrel boy.

"Well, I'm just a bit flustered and out of breath," explained Aunt Lettie. "And my heart is palpitating a bit. It always does when I get excited, and I think you will admit that it is exciting to be walking quietly along the street when, without rhyme or reason, your bonnet is suddenly pulled from your head. It's a good thing I don't wear false curls. But isn't that enough to excite any goat lady?" and she looked sharply at Johnnie.

"Yes, sir—I mean yes'm—it is," agreed the squirrel boy. "But I didn't mean to do it."

"No, I understand that," said Aunt Lettie politely, and with a kind smile. "It wasn't altogether your fault. Boys must play. However, as I am feeling better now, Johnnie, I may as well help you fly your kite."

"Oh, will you really do that?" eagerly asked the little squirrel boy.

"Yes, I will," was the answer.

Aunt Lettie put on her bonnet again, and held the toy of paper, string and sticks so Johnnie could run with the long cord.

"Now let go when I tell you to!" chattered the squirrel boy, and, a moment later he cried: "Let go!"

Well, Aunt Lettie did, but the wind whisked the tail of the kite around her bonnet once more, and pulled it off, though Johnnie caught it before it fell in the dirt.

"Oh, this is getting worse and worse!" bleated Aunt Lettie.

"But the worst is yet to come," whispered a grillery-growlery voice in the deep weeds at the side of the road.

However, neither Aunt Lettie nor Johnnie heard this.

"I'm sorry I spoke so crossly to Uncle Wiggily," said the goat lady, when she had her bonnet again. "I must ask him to forgive me when he returns."

"He's coming now," chattered Johnnie. "He has something Mrs. Twistytail borrowed from Nurse Jane, and forgot to bring back."

Uncle Wiggily came hopping along, and he was wondering what he could say to the goat lady to make her less angry about having her bonnet snatched off by the kite's tail, when Aunt Lettie, with a loud bleat, suddenly cried:

"Oh, Uncle Wiggily! Look! Look behind you!"

But before anything could be done, ALL OF A SUDDEN, out of the weeds jumped the bad laughing Hyena and caught the rabbit uncle, shouting: "Now I have you!"

But Uncle Wiggily had Nurse Jane's coffee grinder which he got from Mr. Twistytail and he caught the front paw of the bad laughing Hyena and said, "I'll grind you all up."

"Oh wow! Please don't! I'll be good!" howled the hyena.

Then the bad animal ran away.

"Oh, how glad I am that you are safe, Uncle Wiggily!" bleated Aunt Lettie. "It's a good thing you thought of going to Mrs. Twistytail's house. I'm so glad!"

"I'm glad, too," chuckled the bunny. "But I'm sorry about your bonnet!"

"Pray do not mention it!" begged the goat lady. "I want to beg your pardon for being so cross! And if you and Johnnie will come to my house I'll give you a piece of pie!"

"Ha! Ha!" chattered the squirrel boy, as he wound up his kite string. "This is the greatest fun yet!" and Uncle Wiggily said the same.

So everything happened for the best; and if the comb doesn't tickle the cake of soap when it's sliding down the wash rag into the bath tub, I'll tell you next about Uncle Wiggily and Tommie's top.

STORY IV

UNCLE WIGGILY AND TOMMIE'S TOP

"OH, Uncle Wiggily! You ought to see it! Come and look—quick!"

This is what Tommy Kat, the pussy boy, was mewing one day in front of the hollow stump bungalow where the rabbit gentleman lived.

"What is it I ought to see, Tommie?" asked Mr. Longears, who was just twinkling his pink nose in front of the looking glass, before starting out to look for an adventure. "What is it?"

"Oh, it's red, white and blue!" went on the pussy boy. "Come on out and look at it Uncle Wiggily while it's going!"

"He must be speaking of my red, white and blue striped barber pole rheumatism crutch," thought the rabbit gentleman. "Tell me where it is going, Tommie! Tell me, that's a good kitten chap!" and Mr. Longears began to get excited.

"It's going around and around!" Tommie answered.

"Oh, my poor red, white and blue rheumatism crutch!" sighed Uncle Wiggily. "It will get dizzy if it goes around so much, and then it will fall down and can't hold me up! Oh, my poor crutch!"

"Ho! Ho!" laughed Tommie Kat. "I wasn't speaking of your barber pole crutch, Uncle Wiggily."

"You weren't?" asked the bunny, hopping out on the front

32

steps of his hollow stump bungalow. "Well, what is going around then?"

"My top!" Tommie replied. "My new top, painted red, white and blue. I just bought it at the store. I wound the string around it, and I spun it in front of your bungalow. That's what I called you out to see—my new top! There she spins!"

Tommie pointed with one paw to something on the sidewalk in front of the rabbit gentleman's hollow stump bungalow. Surely enough it was a spinning top, whizzing around as fast as an electric fan.

"My goodness!" exclaimed Uncle Wiggily, sitting down on the top step. "I was quite excited for a moment, Tommie. I thought the Wild Bull, or perhaps the Laughing Hyena, had taken my rheumatism crutch away. Not that I need it just now," said the bunny, "because I don't—my rheumatism isn't hurting me to-day. But I might have a use for my red, white and blue crutch at any other time. I'm glad it isn't trying to act like a top."

"Would you like to spin my top?" asked Tommie politely, as his toy stopped whizzing and toppled over on its side as if going to sleep. "I came over on purpose to show it to you, and, if you like, you may spin it, Uncle Wiggily."

"Thank you," responded the bunny gentleman. "I'd like to, but——"

He turned half around, looked carefully at his bungalow and seemed to be listening.

"What's the matter?" asked Tommie, sort of anxious like. "Did you think you heard the Fuzzy Fox?"

"No, but I thought I heard Nurse Jane, and I'd rather—
if it's all the same to you, Tommie my boy—I'd just as soon—
not to put too fine a point on it—I'd a little prefer that Nurse
Jane didn't see me spinning a top."

"Yes, I guess she would laugh!" agreed Tommie. "But
she isn't coming."

"No, I believe not," spoke the bunny, relieved like in his
mind. "Hand me the top, Tommie Kat, and I'll try just one
spin. It's been many a year since I had a top in my paw.
When I was a young rabbit I was considered one of the best
top spinners in Animal Land. Let me see what I can do now."

Tommie handed Uncle Wiggily the new red, white and
blue top, and also gave the bunny the string to wind around
the spinning top. Just as Mr. Longears was going to throw
the top, quickly pulling back the string from around it to
make it whirl, Nurse Jane's voice from within the bungalow
called:

"Don't forget what I told you, Wiggy!"

Uncle Wiggily slowly lowered the paw he had raised to
throw the top, and a disappointed look came over the bunny's
face.

"What's the matter," whispered Tommie. "Did she tell
you not to spin any tops?"

"No," answered Uncle Wiggily. "She told me to go on an
errand to get something for her, and I was forgetting all about
it. Your new top made me forget."

"Well spin it once now," urged Tommie, "and then you
can go get what Nurse Jane told you to."

"I know a better way than that!" chuckled the bunny.

"What?" asked Tommie.

"You come with me on the errand," proposed Mr. Long-ears, "and on the way I can spin the top. Then Nurse Jane won't see me and say I'm having my second childhood, or something like that. Ha! Ha! That's what we'll do! I'll take you on the errand with me—I have to get something from the store—but on the way there will be plenty of time to do some top-spinning!"

"Yes, that will be fun!" laughed Tommie. "Come on!"

Together Uncle Wiggily and the pussy boy hurried from in front of the hollow stump bungalow. As they hastened down the street Nurse Jane called again:

"Don't forget to bring back what I told you to get, Wiggy!"

"I'll bring it!" promised the bunny rabbit.

Around the corner went Uncle Wiggily and Tommie. They reached a smooth place on the sidewalk, and the rabbit said:

"This will be a good place to spin the top. Let me try it now."

Once more on the top he wound the string. He raised the top high in the air, and threw it down, suddenly pulling back his paw so as to unwind the string and set the top to spinning.

But something went wrong. Either Uncle Wiggily threw the top too hard or he didn't toss it hard enough. For it bounced up from the sidewalk, instead of spinning, and just then Dr. Possum happened to be passing.

"Bang!" went the top, hitting Dr. Possum in the back.

"Hello there!" cried the animal doctor in great surprise. "Who's doing that?"

Just as he turned around to look, Uncle Wiggily dropped the top cord near where the top had fallen.

"Who hit me?" asked Dr. Possum.

"It—er—it happened to be *Tommie's top*," answered the bunny, blinking one eye at the pussy boy, which was meant for Tommie to keep quiet.

"Well, Tommie, you must be more careful how you spin your top," said Dr. Possum kindly. "You might have made it strike me on my nose, and so have broken my glasses. Please be more careful!"

"Why—er—I—er—I didn't——" began the kitten chap.

But Dr. Possum hurried on, for he was going to give some medicine to Arabella Chick, the hen girl, who had swallowed a grain of corn the wrong way. So Dr. Possum didn't hear what Tommie tried to say.

"Why, he must think I really spun that top!" cried Tommie to Uncle Wiggily. "And *you* did it, and *you* made it bang him!"

"Hush! Don't let him hear you!" chuckled the bunny. "I'll tell him myself later on. If he thought I was spinning tops at my age he'd give me castor oil, maybe, tell Nurse Jane and—well, no matter! Let me have another try, Tommie. I feel sure I'll spin it this time!"

Tommie stood for a moment looking up at Uncle Wiggily, who was holding out his paw for the top and string, which the kitten boy had picked up after the bunny gentleman had let go of them. Uncle Wiggily's pink nose was twinkling rather on one side than straight in the middle, as it was supposed to do.

"Come on, Tommie, let's have the top and string again, and I'll show you some spinning that you'll be proud of," went on the bunny gentleman.

But Tommie held the top and string in his paws behind his back.

"I don't want to be impolite, Uncle Wiggily," mewed the pussy boy, "but I'm afraid if I let you take my top again that you'll get into worse trouble."

Uncle Wiggily looked at the kitten boy for a moment, and then said: "Perhaps you are right, Tommie my lad. Just stay around here. I'll be back in a little while."

"Where are you going?" asked Tommie.

"I'm going to take a few lessons in top spinning," was the answer.

"Where?" mewed Tommie.

"Oh, I'll find a place," exclaimed the bunny gentleman.

Uncle Wiggily hopped along until he came to a little house made of white birch bark. On the door was a sign reading:

LESSONS GIVEN HERE

"I wonder if they give top-spinning lessons?" thought the rabbit uncle. "I'll hop up and ask."

A little old monkey gentleman opened the door when Uncle Wiggily knocked, and the bunny asked:

"Could you teach me to spin a top? You'll have to do it quickly, for Tommie may not wait very long."

"Of course I can teach you to spin a top!" chattered the monkey gentleman. "Come in!"

In hopped the bunny. The monkey gentleman used to keep a toy store, so he knew all about tops, and soon he was giving

Uncle Wiggily a lesson in how to wind the string around the top, throw it down hard, pull back the string with a snappy jerk and set the top to whizzing.

"I believe I can do it now!" chuckled Uncle Wiggily, after

"BANG!"

much practice. He hopped back to where he had left Tommie, near the house of Grandfather Goosey Gander. "Let me take the top now," begged the bunny. "I've had some lessons and I'm sure I am now a good spinner."

Once more Uncle Wiggily wound up the top. Again he

threw it toward the ground, pulling back the string. But the cord caught around the iron point of the top, the top swung over Uncle Wiggily's head and went through Grandpa Goosey Gander's stained glass window—"Bang!"

"Oh, me! Oh, my!" exclaimed Uncle Wiggily. "Here, Tommie, take the top string. I must hurry to do that errand for Nurse Jane! I have to get something she wants very much! I'll be back in a little while!"

And before Tommie could stop him, away ran the bunny gentleman to get what Nurse Jane had asked him to bring her.

Grandfather Goosey Gander came to the door. He looked at his broken window, next he peered at the top which he had picked up inside the room, and then he glanced at Tommie who was holding the top string.

"Tommie," said the gander gentleman, "I thought you knew how to spin tops better than to throw them so they break windows! I'm surprised at you!"

"Oh, Grandpa!" mewed poor Tommie, quite excited. "I didn't—I didn't——"

"Tommie — Tommie! Be careful!" warned Grandpa Goosey, raising one wing. "Count ten before you speak!"

Tommie didn't want to tell on Uncle Wiggily, but he didn't want to bear the blame himself, and he hardly knew what to do. For surely it looked (with him holding the string as he was doing, and no one else in sight) as if he had broken the window.

But just then Uncle Wiggily came hopping back with something Nurse Jane had asked him to get.

"Oh, Grandpa Goosey!" cried the bunny, "please don't

blame Tommie! It was all my fault; just the same as it was my fault that I hit Dr. Possum with the top, and——"

"Speaking of tops," quickly growled a savage voice from behind a big stone, "I think I'll nibble the tops of Uncle Wiggily's ears!"

"What's that?" quacked Grandpa Goosey.

"I don't know!" gasped the bunny.

"Look! Look!" mewed Tommie. "Look what's coming!"

And then, ALL OF A SUDDEN, from behind a tree jumped the bad Skeezicks yelling, "Now I have you!"

"Please let me go," begged the bunny, as he stuck the end of the feather duster, which Nurse Jane had sent him for, right into the face of the Skeezicks.

"Stop tickling me!" howled the Skeezicks.

"That's what feather dusters are for!" laughed Uncle Wiggily.

"Dear me!" quacked Grandpa Goosey when the bad animal had run away, frightened by what the bunny had done to him! "I'm glad he's gone!"

"So am I!" chuckled Uncle Wiggily. "And I must go and tell Dr. Possum that it was I, and not Tommie, who banged him with the top."

"Do you want to try any more spins?" asked the pussy boy.

"Not now, thank you," laughed Mr. Longears. "I guess my top days are over! I'm going back to my bungalow, after I apologize to Dr. Possum, and read the paper."

So the bunny did this, very glad, indeed, that his ears were not nibbled. And if the trolley car doesn't chase the policeman up a tree, so he can't eat chocolate cake with the letter carrier, I'll tell you next about Uncle Wiggily and Jackie's bone.

STORY V

UNCLE WIGGILY AND JACKIE'S BONE

ONCE upon a time, as Uncle Wiggily was hopping through the woods near the Orange Ice Mountains, not far from his hollow stump bungalow, the bunny rabbit gentleman heard a rustling in the bushes.

"Oh dear me!" whispered Mr. Longears to himself, crouching down behind a stone, "I hope this isn't the Bob Cat or the Skillery Scallery Alligator! I have nothing to frighten them away with, for I haven't had a chance to go to the nine and ten cent store to get what Nurse Jane wanted. Oh, what shall I do?"

Uncle Wiggily was looking for a place to hide, when the rustling noise in the bushes sounded again, and a voice cried:

"You'd better hurry if you don't want to be late!"

"Um—um!" thought the bunny gentleman, trying to crouch down beneath some dried leaves. "That sounds rather scary! Maybe the Fuzzy Fox is calling the Woozie Wolf not to be late for a little party they hope to have in nibbling my ears! I must keep very quiet, and perhaps they will pass me by!"

So the bunny kept very quiet, and no bad animals seemed to be coming along. But the voice said again:

"Give me your ears!" growled
the Tiger. "I want some nibbles!"

See page 60.

"Please hurry, Jackie Bow Wow, or you'll be late for school; and you know the lady mouse teacher will make you stay in!"

"Oh, ho! I guess I'm all right after all!" chuckled Uncle Wiggily, as he shook off the leaves and hopped out on the path. "This must be Peetie Bow Wow calling to his brother Jackie. They are on their way to the hollow stump school. I have nothing to fear from my friends the Bow Wow puppy dog boys. But I must see what this means about Jackie being late!"

Coming along through the woods was a little puppy chap, with a bundle of books in a strap. This little dog kept looking back on the forest path every now and then.

"What's the matter, Peetie?" asked the bunny gentleman.

"Oh, it's my brother Jackie," was the answer. "We started for school together, but he keeps lagging behind, and I know he'll be late. The lady mouse teacher may think it's my fault!"

"Well, you trot along," advised Mr. Longears. "Don't you be late, Peetie, whatever happens. I'll hop back there and see if I can hurry Jackie. Something may have happened to him, or perhaps he doesn't know his lessons, and is afraid to go to school."

"Oh, we both know our lessons!" barked Peetie. "To-day we have reading, and Jackie is always good at that. I can't think what's keeping him!"

"I'll hurry him up," said Uncle Wiggily. "You trot along!"

So the one little puppy dog chap hastened to school, while

the bunny rabbit gentleman hopped back on the path to see what was the matter with Jackie.

It took only a short time for Mr. Longears to reach a little mossy-green dingly-dell in the woods—a place where some trees stood in a circle around a fern-bordered spring. And

"Oh, have you found it?" barked the puppy chap

there was Jackie Bow Wow walking backward and forward with his nose to the ground.

"What's the matter, Jackie?" asked Uncle Wiggily.

"Oh, have you found it? Please tell me that you have found it!" barked the puppy dog chap.

"Found what?" asked Uncle Wiggily. "I haven't had

time to find anything yet—I haven't even been to the store to get something for Nurse Jane that she told me to be sure and not forget. Why, have you lost anything, Jackie?"

"Lost anything? I should say I have!" cried the puppy. "I have lost the most lovely, juicy bone you ever saw! I was carrying it to school——"

"Not to gnaw in class, I hope!" interrupted Uncle Wiggily.

"Oh, no indeed!" barked Jackie. "I was only going to gnaw the bone at recess. But now I can't."

"Why not?" Mr. Longears wanted to know.

"Because I've lost it," was the answer. "I mean I've lost my bone, Uncle Wiggily—not my recess."

"I understand," spoke the bunny. "But where did you lose your bone, Jackie?"

"I had it in my strap with my books," explained the puppy chap. "It was a clean bone, so it wouldn't soil the books. I was walking with my brother Peetie, when I happened to see a pretty flower I wanted to pick for the lady mouse teacher.

"I stopped, nibbled off the flower and then I went on again, running fast to catch up to Peetie. But I hadn't gone very far before I missed the bone. I've looked all over for it, but I can't find it. And I know I'll be so hungry at recess, and I'll have nothing to gnaw, and Peetie won't have either, for I was going to let him chew on my bone for a while! Oh dear!" and Jackie whined most pitifully.

"Don't feel so badly about it!" said kind Uncle Wiggily. "Did you look around the place where you picked the flower for the lady mouse teacher?"

"No, I didn't look there," Jackie admitted.

"Well, that's very likely where your bone will be found," went on Mr. Longears. "We'll look there."

"But if I wait any longer I'll be late for school!" whined the puppy chap. "Peetie went on a long time ago!"

"I'll go to school with you and explain to the lady mouse teacher how it happened," promised the bunny gentleman. "Come now, I'll help you look for your bone."

"Oh, thank you!" barked Jackie, and he led the way back to the place where he had put his books and bone down on the ground to pick the pretty flower for the teacher.

"See! There isn't any bone here!" barked Jackie, as he and Uncle Wiggily reached the place.

Truly there was no bone in sight, but the bunny gentleman did not give up so easily. He looked all around and soon he found a hole.

Looking down into the hole Uncle Wiggily cried:

"I see your bone, Jackie. It either fell down this hole by itself, or some bad animal dragged it in there to hide it!"

"Oh, my!" barked the puppy. "I hope there are no bad animals here, Uncle Wiggily!" He looked around the bushes, but no danger seemed near.

"I don't believe any bad chaps will be out so early in the morning," Uncle Wiggily said, hopeful like.

"But how are we going to get my bone?" asked Jackie, anxiously.

"We must dig it up out of the hole," answered Mr. Longears. "If I had a hoe, a rake or even Nurse Jane's stove poker I might lift the bone up that way. Or I could do it with my red, white and blue striped rheumatism crutch, only I haven't that with me. I left it near your books. The only way is to dig down, make the hole larger and then we can easily reach the bone. We are both good diggers with our paws, Jackie. Come on! We'll dig up your bone!"

So they started, Uncle Wiggily on one side of the hole and Jackie on the other. My, how they made the dirt fly! Some little ants, living near the hole, crawled out to see what was going on.

"We'll help!" offered the kind ants. "We'll help!"

"Pooh! Ants can't help dig for a big bone!" objected Jackie.

"Perhaps they can't help dig," said Uncle Wiggily, giving Jackie a little pinch on his tail to warn him to be more polite. "But they can carry away the grains of dirt that we dig out with our paws."

"That's what we'll do," agreed the ants, and as there were about five million of them they helped very much in carrying away the grains of dirt as fast as they were loosened from around the hole.

Uncle Wiggily and Jackie were digging away, getting nearer and nearer to the doggie's bone, when the bunny said:

"This is going to take longer than I thought, Jackie. You surely will be late for school, I'm afraid. I have to go to the store, to get something for Nurse Jane, and on my way I'll stop and tell the lady mouse teacher that you'll come along as soon as you can, after you get your bone. You keep on digging, and I'll hop to the store and also to the hollow stump school." And Uncle Wiggily twinkled his pink nose.

"All right," answered Jackie, and he thought it rather fun to stay out of class to dig up his lost bone.

Uncle Wiggily soon hopped to the store, bought what Nurse Jane had asked him to get for her, and then he made a few jumps to the hollow stump school. The lady mouse teacher was very kind about it.

"Tell Jackie it will be all right," she squeaked. "I won't mark him late. Let him come to school as soon as he gets his recess-bone."

Uncle Wiggily hopped back to the green, mossy dell. Just as he reached it, carrying what Nurse Jane had asked him to buy for her, Jackie finally dug down to the bottom of the hole and pulled up his bone.

"Ah! Here it is!" barked the doggie boy. "Now I'll have fun!"

"What are you going to do?" asked Uncle Wiggily, giving his pink nose just the least little bit of a twinkle.

"Well, first I'm going to gnaw this bone a bit," answered the doggie boy.

Jackie held the bone down on the ground between his two paws, as you have often seen dogs do, and then he started to gnaw, his strong, white teeth rasping on the bone.

All of a sudden Jackie stopped gnawing.

"What's the matter?" asked Uncle Wiggily. "Do you hear a funny noise? Do you think the Pipsisewah or Skeezicks is coming?"

"Oh, no indeed!" laughingly barked Jackie. "Nothing like that. But I just happened to think it wasn't very polite for me to start gnawing away on my bone without offering you some."

"Offering me some what?" asked the bunny.

"Some of my bone," went on Jackie. "It was very impolite of me, and I hope you'll forgive me. Will you have a nibble?" and, taking the bone in his teeth, Jackie walked across the green, grassy place to where Uncle Wiggily stood.

"Oh, thank you! No!" laughed the bunny. "We rabbits don't gnaw bones though we often gnaw the bark off trees. No, indeed, Jackie, eat all you wish from your bone. You aren't a bit impolite in not offering me any. But how long are you going to stay here?" asked Uncle Wiggily.

"Oh, just long enough to take a few more nibbles," answered Jackie. "Why, is there any hurry?"

"Well," spoke Uncle Wiggily, and there was a funny little twinkle in his eyes as well as on the end of his pink nose. "You know, Jackie, you started for school, and losing the bone, and finding it again, aren't really part of your school work. The lady mouse teacher said you might stay away from your class long enough to find the bone, but, now that you have it, I think you'd better trot along to the hollow stump; don't you?"

"Oh, I just want to have a little more fun!" barked Jackie. "Oh, I know what we can do!" he suddenly yelped.

"What?" asked the bunny uncle. "If you mean that I can hear your lessons here in the woods, I'm not going to do it. You should go to school."

"No, it isn't that!" laughed Jackie. "But this is what we can do to have fun. We can play ball with my bone. That you can do, even if you don't like to gnaw the bone. Come on, we'll have a catch—we'll make believe the bone is a base-ball."

"You can think up more ways of keeping out of school than any one I ever saw," said Uncle Wiggily. "Just wait a moment until I put over on this stump the thing I got for Nurse Jane. Then you and I will have a catch and——"

"Yes, and I'll have Uncle Wiggily!" quickly cried another voice.

Jackie looked up and saw something that made him shout: "Run, Uncle Wiggily! Run!"

But it was too late.

And then, ALL OF A SUDDEN, out from behind the stump jumped the Woozie Wolf and caught Uncle Wiggily.

But Uncle Wiggily turned the egg beater against the nose of the Woozie Wolf and said, "Have an egg-beater shampoo, Mr. Wolf."

Away ran the bad animal, for he didn't dare stay when Uncle Wiggily acted so bravely, and not an ear nibble did the unpleasant chap get.

"Now everything is all right!" barked Jackie, as he strapped the bone in with his books again, and started for school, not forgetting to thank the ants who had helped him.

"Yes, everything is all right," agreed the rabbit gentleman. "And it's a good thing I went to the store for Nurse Jane before coming back to help you dig up your bone. Now run along to your class, Jackie. Everything is all right and the lady mouse teacher will not mark you late."

"Thank you," said Jackie as he went to school with his bone. And if the broom doesn't try to slide down the cellar steps on the bread tray, and scatter cake crumbs down the back of the gold fish, I'll tell you next about Uncle Wiggily and Lulu Wibblewobble.

STORY VI

UNCLE WIGGILY AND LULU WIBBLEWOBBLE

"ARE you going to need anything from the store to-day, Nurse Jane?" asked Uncle Wiggily one morning, as he was getting ready to hop away from his hollow stump bungalow, to go look for an adventure. "Will you need a cake of soap or a slice of cheese?"

"Neither one, I think, but thank you just the same," answered the muskrat lady. "I don't believe—Oh, yes there is, too!" she went on quickly. "I was nearly forgetting. I do need something from the store. Wait a moment until I think what it is."

Nurse Jane combed out her whiskers, which she always did when she was thinking, and then she squeaked:

"Now I remember what it was! Here, I'll write it down for you on this little piece of white birch bark so you won't forget."

With a burned match for a pencil, Nurse Jane wrote on the white birch bark the name of something she wanted Uncle Wiggily to bring her from the eleven and twelve cent store when he came back.

"Don't forget now!" begged the muskrat lady housekeeper.

"I'll remember," promised the bunny, thrusting the bit of bark in his pocket.

Away Uncle Wiggily hopped, over the fields and through

the woods wondering what sort of adventure he would have that day.

"I seem to be rather lucky of late," said Mr. Longears to himself, twinkling his pink nose a little upside down for a change. "I have been able to drive away all the bad chaps that tried to catch me to nibble my ears. And all on account of the things I happen to get for Nurse Jane.

"I wonder what I am to bring her to-day, and what bad animal I shall drive away with it?" mused the bunny as he hopped along.

He had not hopped very far before he suddenly heard a sort of whistling noise in the weeds and something whizzed up in front of the bunny, sailed along and cried:

"There, you didn't win!"

"Didn't win what?" asked Uncle Wiggily in surprise. "I wasn't trying to win anything."

"You weren't?" exclaimed the other, and by this time the bunny saw that it was a big green grasshopper who had loomed up from the weeds just in front of the rabbit. "Excuse me, but I thought you were racing hops with me and trying to win. No matter, I'll sail along and find a hop toad to race with." And away sailed the green chap.

"That was very funny," said the bunny.

Uncle Wiggily was going to put his paw in his pocket and take out the bit of white birch bark to read what was written on it when, all of a sudden, a voice behind him asked:

"Are you going with me?"

Uncle Wiggily gave such a jump that he nearly lost the twinkle from the end of his pink nose.

"Oh, my goodness!" cried the bunny, getting ready to run. "Is this the Leopard or the Gorilla who wants me to come with them?"

"Ha! Ha!" laughed a quacking voice. "It isn't either of those bad animals, Uncle Wiggily! I just want to know if you are coming to watch me swim!"

"Lulu Wibble!" gasped Mr. Longears

"Lulu Wibblewobble!" gasped Mr. Longears, turning around so suddenly that he sat down rather hard. But there happened to be some soft moss on the ground, and he wasn't hurt.

"Yes, I'm Lulu," cheerfully quacked the duck girl. "I s'pose you didn't know me 'cause I have on my new hair ribbon," she added with a laugh, as she flapped the red-pink-green bow around her head.

"Well, partly that," admitted Uncle Wiggily, sort of trying to catch his breath, which had nearly run away from him. "But I think I was a bit startled also—not to put it more plainly, and say frightened."

"Why?" asked the duck girl. "What frightened you?"

"I—I thought perhaps you might be the Pipsisewah or the Skeezicks," replied the bunny.

"Oh ho!" laughed Lulu. "Do I look like either of those bad animals—especially with my new red-pink-green hair ribbon? Do I?"

"No," slowly answered Uncle Wiggily, "I can't say that you do. But where did you say you were going, Lulu?"

"To swim in the duck pond. Don't you want to come and watch me? I know you don't care for swimming yourself, as it makes your fur all wet, but this is a hot day and it will cool you to watch me swim," quacked the duck girl.

"I believe it will," agreed Mr. Longears. "I have to go to the store to get something for Nurse Jane," he said, feeling the bit of birch bark in his pocket, "but that will do later. First I'll come and see you swim."

Uncle Wiggily and Lulu Wibblewobble were going through the woods together when, all at once, they heard a sad little voice saying:

"Oh, dear! Oh, dear! Oh, dear!"

"That sounds like trouble!" quacked Lulu.

"I am in trouble!" went on the voice, and it was so sad and

gentle that Uncle Wiggily knew it could be no bad animal trying to nip his ears.

"Where are you?" asked the bunny gentleman.

"Right down here on the ground," was the answer. "I am a poor old hop toad lady. One of my legs is caught under a stone, and I can't get it out. And, even if I could pull my leg from beneath the stone, I'm afraid I'll be so lame that I can't hop for a week! Oh, what shall I do? Oh, dear! Oh, dear! Oh, dear!"

"We'll help you," kindly offered the bunny. "Lulu, take hold with your yellow bill and pull on one side of the stone, while I lift it on the other side. We'll raise it off the hop toad lady's leg."

This the bunny and the little girl duck did, and soon Mrs. Toad was free. But, just as she had feared, her leg was so sore and lame that she could not hop on it.

"How am I ever to get home?" she croaked.

"On my back, of course!" quickly quacked Lulu. "I have a broad back, covered with soft feathers. I'll ride you home on my back."

"I might fall off!" sighed the hop toad lady, who was very nervous.

"I'll hold you on," kindly offered Uncle Wiggily. So he walked beside Lulu, holding the toad lady on the girl duck's back, and soon they were at the house where Mrs. Toad lived. They helped her in, and called Dr. Possum. Then, with the toad lady still calling her thanks to them, Uncle Wiggily and Lulu went down to the duck pond.

"Now watch me swim!" quacked Lulu.

Into the water she splashed and began paddling about with her webbed feet, which were just made for swimming.

"I'll sit on the bank and watch you," said Uncle Wiggily.

It was cool and quiet on the shady shore of the duck pond, and, almost before he knew it, Uncle Wiggily was falling asleep. And, as he slept, the piece of white birch bark slipped from his pocket and tickled his paw.

"Oh, ho!" suddenly exclaimed the rabbit gentleman, rousing himself with a start. "This will never do! I came nearly forgetting that Nurse Jane wanted me to get her something from the store. I must go get it before I fall completely asleep."

"Oh, Uncle Wiggily! Aren't you going to stay and watch me swim?" quacked Lulu, who was going in a circle like a merry-go-'round. "I'm going to do some tricks pretty soon— standing on my head and waving my paddle-feet in the air is one trick!"

"I'd like to see that," said the bunny. "But just now I happened to remember that I promised Nurse Jane to get her something from the store. I don't quite know what it is, but I have it written down on this bit of birch bark. And, even if I haven't my glasses, the little mousie clerk in the store will read it for me.

"So I'll toddle on, get what Nurse Jane needs and when I come back I'll watch you swim some more," promised Uncle Wiggily.

"Please do," begged Lulu. "I'll be ready with my tricks, then."

Away hopped Uncle Wiggily to the store, getting what

Nurse Jane had asked him to bring her. With it he hopped back to the duck pond where he had left Lulu.

As he reached the shore, Uncle Wiggily saw Lulu out in the middle of the pond with her feet in the air, and her head under the water. Of course Uncle Wiggily couldn't see Lulu's head, as it was below the surface, but he knew her head must be there, as Lulu couldn't wobble her feet if she had lost her head. And her feet were wobbling, and wobbling very fast indeed!

"Oh fine, Lulu! Fine!" cried the bunny, clapping his paws. "That's a very good trick! Bravo!"

But Lulu never raised her head and she never quacked a word in answer.

"Good! Oh, very good!" cried the bunny more loudly this time, for he thought, Lulu's head being under water, perhaps she had not heard him. "Well done! But I think that's enough. You'll be all out of breath if you stay down there much longer! Come on out!"

Still Lulu never quacked a sound, but Uncle Wiggily saw her feet wobbling faster than ever, and then he noticed some air bubbles coming up in the water around her neck.

"Oh, my goodness!" shouted the bunny. "I know what has happened! Lulu did her trick of standing upside down. She rammed her head into the soft, mushy, mucky mud on the bottom of the pond, and she's stuck! She can't get loose! She's stuck in the mud as Sammie was with his new boots! I must save Lulu!"

The bunny gentleman was doing his best to think of a quick way to save the little duck girl. He knew it would have to be a quick way, for when one is stuck in the mud with one's head under water there can't be too much quickness.

"Here I come!" cried Uncle Wiggily, hopping toward the pond.

"Hi! What's the matter? What's going on?" suddenly asked a boy's voice. "Is there a ball game?"

"No indeed," answered Uncle Wiggily. "I only wish it were a ball game. But look at poor Lulu, stuck in the mud, with her head under water. I must save her. But who are you?"

As if in answer, out of the bushes came Joie Kat, the pussy brother of Tommie and Kittie Kat.

"If I only had a kite, like the one you helped the squirrel boy to fly, I could save Lulu," mewed Joie.

"How?" asked the bunny.

"Well, I could fly the kite out over the pond right above Lulu's head. Then I could pay out on the string until the kite went down low enough so Lulu could grab the tail in her wings and I'll pull her out."

"But she's upside down!" cried Uncle Wiggily. "That's the trouble! She can't see to grab anything. What I need is something long that I can reach out to the duck girl. I need something like a clothes pole. I wonder if I couldn't find something?"

Uncle Wiggily looked around, found a long tree branch with which he could reach Lulu while he was still standing on shore, and with the branch the bunny poked in the mud on the pond bottom until he had loosened it so the duck girl could pull up her head.

"Oh! Oh my!" gasped Lulu, taking a long breath and shaking herself all over. "I thought you would never save me, Uncle Wiggily!" She wobbled her tail sideways.

"Well, at first I thought you were just doing a trick," said the bunny gentleman. "But when you stayed upside down so long I knew it wasn't a trick, and——"

"Speaking of tricks—how's this?" suddenly shouted a most unpleasant voice. There was a rustling in the bushes. Lulu quacked:

"Oh, look out, Uncle Wiggily! Look out!"

Then, ALL OF A SUDDEN out of the bushes jumped a bad tiger, growling, "Give me your ears! I want some nibbles!"

Uncle Wiggily had the tea kettle, Nurse Jane had asked him to bring her, and he poured hot water on the bad tiger.

"Ha! Ha! I guess he thinks this tea kettle is a new kind of gun," laughed Uncle Wiggily.

And when Uncle Wiggily had done this, away ran the bad chap, howling and yowling and making all sorts of noises because he couldn't nibble any ears.

"My! How brave you are!" quacked Lulu, as she washed the mud off her head. "You rescued me and saved yourself!"

"Just luck," spoke the bunny, modest like and unassuming. "Nothing but luck! If I hadn't gone to the store to get what Nurse Jane wanted, things might not have turned out as they did. And now, Lulu, what other swimming tricks can you do?"

"I don't believe I want to do any more now," answered the duck girl. "I'm tired. Let's go home!"

"Yes, I expect Nurse Jane is waiting for me," said Mr. Longears.

So away went the two friends off through the woods, happy and jolly; and if the canary bird doesn't take one of its feathers and tickle the face of the clock so it waves its hands at the looking glass, I'll tell you next about Uncle Wiggily and Buddy Pigg.

STORY VII

UNCLE WIGGILY AND BUDDY PIGG

UNCLE WIGGILY hopped down the steps of his hollow stump bungalow one morning, and the bunny rabbit gentleman was just going to skip along the path that led to the woods, when he heard a bell ringing.

"That can't be the dinner bell," thought Mr. Longears to himself, "for I've just had breakfast. It isn't the front door bell, for I am right here and I see no one at the door. We have no back door bell—everyone who comes there knocks. So it must be the telephone."

And it was the telephone bell.

"Tinkle! Tinkle! Ting!" it rang again.

"Oh, well, Nurse Jane is in the bungalow. She will answer," thought Uncle Wiggily. "But I had better wait and see if I am wanted."

The bunny gentleman sat himself down on the top step and waited. He was wondering what sort of an adventure he might have in the woods that day, and he was trying to guess which of the bad animals might jump out and try to catch him when, all at once, he heard Nurse Jane speaking to him from an open window.

"Oh, Wiggy!" called the muskrat lady housekeeper. "Have you gone adventuring yet?"

"No, I'm right here—waiting to see what that telephone was ringing for," answered Mr. Longears.

"I'm glad you waited," spoke Miss Fuzzy Wuzzy. "That was Mrs. Stubtail, the lady bear. She telephoned to ask me to have you stop in if you passed her house to-day."

"I shall be most happy to pay a visit to Mrs. Stubtail," laughed Uncle Wiggily, with a low and polite bow. "Is it about anything special she wants me to call? Is Neddie or Beckie Stubtail ill, and does she want me to amuse the children bears?"

"Oh, no," replied Nurse Jane. "It isn't anything like that. But Mrs. Stubtail telephoned to say that she borrowed something from me last week, and she wants to send it back by you, if you'll be so kind as to stop and get it."

"Of course I will," agreed Uncle Wiggily. "But what is it she borrowed that she wants me to bring back?"

"I can't imagine," answered the muskrat lady housekeeper, as she brushed a little dust off the window sill with the end of her tail. "The only thing I remember lending Mrs. Stubtail was a pair of silk stockings and some sugar, and——"

"Maybe she'll put the sugar in the stockings and I can carry both back very easily that way!" chuckled the bunny.

"Nonsense! The very idea!" cried Nurse Jane. "No, now that I think of it, Mrs. Stubtail paid me back the sugar and brought over the silk stockings last week. It must be something else she borrowed, but I can't think what it was. Anyhow, Wiggy my dear, stop at the lady bear's house and get whatever she has to send back to me."

"I will," promised the bunny uncle. "And now may I go adventuring?" he asked, politely.

"Yes," graciously answered Miss Fuzzy Wuzzy, and away hopped the bunny rabbit.

Over the fields and through the woods Uncle Wiggily hurried, for he was a little late and he was becoming quite anxious to see what adventure might be waiting for him that morning.

All at once he heard a queer, buzzing sound near some bushes, and a little voice cried:

"Oh, let me out! Please help me out!"

"That must be a little teeny-weeny fairy," said Uncle Wiggily, looking about, "for I see no one who could talk like that."

"You can't see me because I am down inside this blue flower," went on the voice, sounding as though it came from some cellar. "Open the blue flower and I'll come out."

At first Uncle Wiggily thought this might be a trick of one of the bad animals. But when he saw the blue flower nodding in the summer breeze near where he stood, and when he noticed how small the blossom was, the bunny said:

"No big, bad animal could get into such a little posy as that. I'll let out whoever is inside there."

Very carefully, so he would not tear the beautiful flower, Uncle Wiggily opened the petals which had become twisted together at the top, making a sort of closed vase. And as soon as this posy-vase was opened out flew a honey bee.

"Oh, thank you, Uncle Wiggily, for having let me out!" buzzed the bee. "I shall now give you a whole drop of honey, all for yourself."

"Thank you," murmured the bunny gentleman as he sipped

the drop of honey off his pink, twinkling nose, where the bee put it. "But how did you get shut up in that flower, if I may ask?"

"Oh, I was flitting around, gathering honey and pollen, which is the yellow dust that we bees use to make wax with," came the answer, "when, all of a sudden, as I was deep inside this flower, the wind twisted the petals tightly shut at the top. I just couldn't open them to get out, and I was so frightened!"

"It wasn't my fault," whispered the blue flower. " I would have opened if I could, and have let you out, Dear Bee—but I couldn't."

"I know," buzzed the Bee. "But Uncle Wiggily came along just in time, and I thank him, and I thank you, Blue Flower, for having given me honey. Now I must gather more and fly back to the hive."

"Well, that was a nice little adventure, but hardly exciting enough," thought Uncle Wiggily, as he hopped along, every now and then stopping to look down at his pink, twinkling nose to see if any more honey had gathered on it. But none had, I am sorry to say.

All of a sudden, just as the bunny gentleman was peering behind a large, green mossy log, he heard a voice saying:

"Oh dear, how thirsty I am!"

"My goodness me sakes alive and a thimble full of ice cream!" exclaimed Uncle Wiggily, holding his paw over his pink nose to stop it from twinkling so fast. "Who was that?"

No one answered except that the same sad voice sighed:

"Oh, how thirsty I am!"

"Well if that's the Bob Cat or the Skillery Scallery Alligator, I'm glad to hear that he's thirsty instead of hungry," thought the bunny uncle. "For, being thirsty, he can't drink my ears, but if he was hungry he might nibble them."

Once again the voice cried:

"Oh, how thirsty I am!"

Still the bunny could see no one, and then, taking courage and getting brave he called:

"Say, if you tell me who you are, and where you are, maybe I can get you a drink of water."

"Oh, if you only could it would be so kind of you!" went on the sad voice. "Well, I am a poor old mud turtle lady, and I live inside this hollow log right near you."

Then, looking inside the log, instead of behind it or in front of it, Uncle Wiggily saw that the fallen tree was hollow, and was made into a little house. And in the tree-house lived a poor old mud turtle lady.

"I'm so old and have so much rheumatism I can't walk," she said; "and to-day my husband went off and forgot to leave me any water to drink. Oh, how thirsty I am!"

"I'll get you a drink," kindly said Uncle Wiggily. So he hopped to the spring, brought some water in a Jack-in-the-pulpit flower and gave it to the mud turtle lady.

"Thank you," she murmured, as Uncle Wiggily made a low and polite bow.

On and on hopped the rabbit gentleman, over more fields and through more woods when, all of a sudden, he heard a rustling in the bushes.

"This sounds like an adventure coming!" whispered Uncle Wiggily. "I wonder what kind it is?"

Then, all at once, the rabbit uncle heard a voice that he well knew sadly crying:

"Oh, let me go! Please let me go! I'll give you all the money in my little tin savings bank if you'll only let me go!"

" Please let me go!"

"No, indeed, I will not let you go!" came a hissing voice in answer, and, for a moment, Uncle Wiggily thought he was near a steam radiator, such as warm cold rooms on frosty mornings. But this was summer, and Uncle Wiggily knew no one, not even a janitor, would have steam hissing out of a radiator on such a warm day.

"I'll take a look and see who this is that wants to be let go," thought the rabbit. Peering through the bushes he saw a sight that made his pink nose twinkle backwards.

For there was Buddy Pigg, the little guinea pig boy, caught in the coils of a big snake. Buddy was trying to get loose and sadly saying:

"Oh, let me go! Please let me go! I'll give you all the money in my little tin savings bank if you'll only let me go!"

"No, indeed!" hissed the snake in answer. "The only way I'll let you go is for you to give me a piece off your tail!"

"But I have no tail!" sobbed Buddy. "We guinea pigs never have any tails. You can see for yourself that I haven't a smitch of a tail!"

"What is that to me?" hissed the snake. "Get a tail then— I don't care where you get it—but get one, give me a piece, and I'll let you go!"

"But where can I get a tail?" wailed Buddy Pigg.

"That's it—where can a guinea pig get a tail when he never had one—when he was born without one?" asked Uncle Wiggily, suddenly hopping out from behind a bush where he had been hiding.

"Pooh! Nonsense! Whoever heard of an animal without a tail?" sneered the snake. "Let him get a tail if he wants me to let him go!"

"Talk about animals with no tail," said Uncle Wiggily. "Look at Bully and Bawly the frogs for instance! They have no tails!"

"Pooh! Nonsense!" snapped the snake. "When those frog boys were little tadpoles they had tails. But when they grew up, and found it wasn't fashionable for frogs to have tails, they just dropped theirs. Now there is no use talking! I am hungry for a bit of tail. I have caught Buddy, and unless he gives me a bit of his tail I'll never let him go, and you can't make me, Mr. Longears! Siss! Siss! Siss!"

Suddenly Uncle Wiggily had an idea.

"If I bring you a piece of a tail will you let Buddy go?" asked the bunny gentleman, cunning like and sly.

"Yes!" hissed the snake. "Bring me a piece of tail."

"All right—wait a minute!" cried the rabbit. Away he hopped to a swamp not far distant. It was near the home of Mrs. Stubtail, the lady bear, and when from her window she saw Uncle Wiggily she called out:

"Oh, you have come to take back what I borrowed from Nurse Jane; haven't you? Here it is and thank her for me," and the bear lady gave Uncle Wiggily back what she had borrowed.

"I didn't come for this, exactly," said the rabbit uncle. "I came here to get one of the cat tail plants growing in the swamp. A snake has caught Buddy Pigg and won't let him go unless he gets a piece of a tail. So I'm going to fool the crawly snake with a bit of brown cat tail! Ha! Ha!"

"Oh, what a good joke!" laughed Mrs. Stubtail. "It will serve that snake just right!"

So Uncle Wiggily picked a brown cat tail, of which many grew in the swamp, and then he hopped back to where the snake had caught poor Buddy. The rabbit uncle took with him what the bear lady had given him to take back to Nurse Jane.

"Here you are, Mr. Snake! Here's a bit of tail for you!" cried Uncle Wiggily, tossing the round, brown bit of cat tail plant to the crawly, scaly creature.

"Ah, that's what I need!" hissed the snake, before he quite saw what it was. "Now don't tell me ever again, Buddy Pigg, that you can't get a tail when you want one!" the snake added, as he uncoiled himself and let the little chap go free.

Over to Uncle Wiggily ran Buddy, and just then a loud voice cried:

"I don't want a tail—I want ears to nibble—Uncle Wiggily's ears! That's what I want!"

"Oh, see what's coming!" cried Buddy, pointing back of the bunny gentleman, and then, ALL OF A SUDDEN, the Skillery Skallery Alligator caught Mr. Longears.

Uncle Wiggily opened the umbrella, the bear lady had given him to take back to Nurse Jane, and stuck it right into the mouth of the Skillery Skallery Alligator.

"Now let's see you bite me," laughed Uncle Wiggily.

"Good, Uncle Wiggily! Good!" cried Buddy Pigg, when he saw what had happened. "That's the way to treat all the bad animals! Good, is what I call it!" and the guinea pig boy laughed as the unpleasant chap hurried off.

"Bad! That's what I call it!" hissed the snake. "Look here! You fooled me!" the crawly creature went on, holding up the cat tail plant. "This is no good! I can't eat this! It's all fluffy and feathery!"

"Well, you didn't say what kind of a tail you wanted!" laughed the bunny, " and I picked the first one I could find to give you. Come on, Buddy!"

And away quickly hopped the bunny gentleman and the little guinea pig chap, while the cross old snake, left far behind, hissed:

"Oh, they fooled me! They fooled me! I can't eat an old, dried cat tail plant!"

But it was all he had for supper, and it served him right, I think. Anyhow if the cow doesn't jump over the moon and forget to leave any cream for the baby mosquito, I'll tell you next about Uncle Wiggily and Arabella Chick.

STORY VIII

UNCLE WIGGILY AND ARABELLA CHICK

ONE day Mrs. Chick, the mother of Charlie and Arabella, the little hen and rooster, said:

"Arabella, I wish you'd go over to Uncle Wiggily's hollow stump bungalow for me."

"Of course I will, Momsie!" cackled Arabella, for she was a good little hen girl. "Do you want him to come over here and play with me?" Arabella asked. "There isn't any school to-day."

"Nonsense!" clucked Mrs. Chick. "Uncle Wiggily is too busy looking after adventures to play with you, or Charlie either. Anyhow, Charlie is off playing ball with the animal boys."

"Well, Uncle Wiggily often plays with us," said Arabella. "That is he does when Nurse Jane doesn't see him to laugh at him."

"Well, it isn't about any play that I am now asking you to go to Uncle Wiggily's bungalow," went on Mrs. Chick. "I have just baked some fresh corn muffins, and as the bunny gentleman is very fond of them I thought I'd send him a few."

"Oh, I shall love to take them to him," cackled the little hen girl. And when her mother had wrapped the muffins in a napkin of clean corn husks, and had placed them in a birch bark basket, Arabella tucked the basket handle under one wing

72

and started off, her hair ribbon fluttering in the summer breeze.

"All the same maybe Uncle Wiggily will play with me, or take me adventuring with him," thought Arabella as she skipped along, sort of playing stone tag, all by herself.

The way to play stone tag, all by yourself, is to hurry along never stepping on a stone. If you *should* happen to step on one, that means you are "it," and you have to hop all the remainder of the way, wherever you are going, by stepping on stones every step you take. If you don't do this it isn't fair.

"It would be more fun if I had some one to play this game with me," thought the little hen girl, as she looked here and there, over and under the bushes for an animal boy or girl with whom she might have fun. But she saw no one. "So I guess I'll have to play by myself," went on Arabella with a little cackle.

But, all of a sudden, she heard a noise in the bushes, right near a green tree that would be ripe and ready to cut down at next Christmas time to hang presents on. And suddenly Arabella saw, perched on the limb of a tree, a robin.

"Do you want to play stone tag with me?" asked Arabella.

"Thank you, dear little hen girl, I would like to play your kind of stone tag, but I must play a different game," sang the robin.

"What sort of a game?" asked Arabella.

"Oh, I must fly away, find some red, ripe cherries, and take the stones out of them so the cherries will be safe for my little birds to eat," chirped the robin. "That is the kind of stone tag I must play."

"Well, that's a good game, too!" laughed Arabella. "But

I haven't time to play that.   I must flutter on, now, to Uncle Wiggily's bungalow."

Well, Arabella was playing stone tag—that is the first part of it—where she had to keep off stones when, all of a sudden,

"Oh, dear me!" cackled the hen girl

she jumped so hard, to flutter over a large stone, that one of the corn muffins bounced out of the birch bark basket.

"Oh, dear me!" cackled the hen girl, and she was so excited that, quite by accident, she stepped on a stone, and then she was "it."

"Now let's see you bite me!"
laughed Uncle Wiggily

See page 70.

"Now I'll have to step on stones all the rest of the way to Uncle Wiggily's," said Arabella to herself. "Well, I don't mind—it will be lots of fun. But I must pick up Uncle Wiggily's corn muffin."

Using her bill, which she wiped clean on a blade of grass, Arabella picked up the corn cake.

"It isn't hurt very much," she said to herself. "Just a little bit broken off one edge. He'll never notice that."

She was about to put it back in the basket with the others when she happened to see a little black pebble sticking in the top of the cake.

"I'll leave that little stone in the muffin," cackled Arabella with a laugh. "It looks like a raisin. Of course I'll tell Uncle Wiggily it isn't really a raisin, else he might bite on it and break off one of his teeth," thought the little hen girl.

So saying, Arabella placed the corn muffin, with the little black pebble make-believe raisin on top, back in the basket, covered all the cakes over with the green corn-husk napkin, and on she fluttered again, playing stone tag.

What Arabella once said about having her teeth in her stomach was quite true. Birds and chickens have no teeth, but they have a gizzard, and inside this gizzard are stones, gravel and perhaps bits of glass. All these serve as teeth to a hen, and all the food goes first into the gizzard, there to be chewed as we chew our food in our mouth.

Arabella felt quite happy as she flittered along, and of course she was very careful always to step on a stone. Because she was "it," you know, from having stepped on a stone by accident while playing tag, and it wouldn't have been fair to go along, now, without stepping on stones every foot of the way.

Playing this game made Arabella a bit late in reaching Uncle Wiggily's hollow stump bungalow, and the rabbit gentleman was just starting out to go look for an adventure when the hen girl, stepping off the last stone to the lowest bungalow step, cackled joyfully:

"Oh, Uncle Wiggily! You can't guess what I have brought you!"

"Well, you have brought me yourself, for one thing," said the bunny with a smile, for he was very glad to see Arabella.

"Oh, but I have brought you something else!" went on Charlie's sister. "Look—some lovely corn muffins my mother baked for you!"

"Fine!" cried Uncle Wiggily. "If there is one thing I like more than another it is corn muffins—except, perhaps, an occasional cherry pie. But cherries aren't in season now. Oh, they're just perfectly *lovificant!*" exclaimed the bunny, as he looked in the basket and saw the muffins.

"What does *lovificant* mean?" asked Arabella, rather puzzled by this new word.

"Well, it means lovely and magnificant all made into one!" chuckled Mr. Longears. "Whenever anything is specially nice I say it is *lovificant*—and that's what these muffins are! I'll eat that one, with a raisin on top, right now!"

"That isn't a raisin!" spoke Arabella, sort of bashful like.

"No?" asked Uncle Wiggily. "It looks like one. Of course I haven't my glasses, but——"

"It's a stone," said Arabella, "asking your pardon for interrupting you. It's a black pebble that stuck in the muffin when I dropped it out of my basket playing stone tag," and she told the truth, you see. In fact she always did.

"Well, one little stone won't harm a muffin," said the bunny in a jolly voice. "I'll eat all around it."

"And it's a bit broken on the edges, too," added Arabella. "I mean this one muffin is—I didn't spill any of the others."

"I don't mind broken edges!" laughed Mr. Longears. "The muffin will be worse broken up than that before I finish eating it," and he began to nibble it.

"Is it good?" asked Arabella, picking up some of the crumbs Uncle Wiggily dropped, for her chicken beak was purposely made for picking up crumbs and small things like that.

"Oh, it's just *lovificant!*" exclaimed Mr. Longears. "I'll only eat this one now. Take the others in to Nurse Jane, Arabella, my dear, and you and I will go off adventuring!"

"Oh, are you going to take me! How perfectly wonderful!" cackled the hen girl. "I was hoping you would, but mother said you might be too busy!"

"Not at all," spoke Uncle Wiggily, with a low polite bow. "Take the muffins in and come along."

"Tell Uncle Wiggily not to forget," said Nurse Jane to Arabella, as the hen child gave the muskrat lady housekeeper the basket.

"Not to forget what?" Arabella wanted to know.

"What I told him to get for me," went on Miss Fuzzy Wuzzy. "He knows all right."

"Nurse Jane says you aren't to forget," cackled Arabella, when she came out and hopped down the bungalow steps.

"I'll remember," promised the bunny uncle. "It's just something she wanted me to bring from the home of Mrs. Kinkytail, the monkey lady—something Nurse Jane has to borrow, as she can't find hers this morning."

"I'll help you not to forget to remember," kindly offered Arabella.

She and Uncle Wiggily hopped on and on, over the fields and through the woods, looking on all sides for adventures. But strange happenings seemed rather scarce that morning.

"I think perhaps we aren't going to find any," Uncle Wiggily was saying when, all of a sudden, a voice cried:

"There you go! Now you've done it! Just look!"

"What's that?" whispered Arabella, snuggling close to Uncle Wiggily. "Oh, what is it?"

"I don't know—an adventure, I hope," replied the bunny. "But first let me take a look—it may be some bad animal trying to play a trick!"

He peered through the bushes as the voice said again:

"All spilled! Every bit of it—every grain!"

"Come on, Arabella!" cried Uncle Wiggily with a jolly laugh. "It is only Johnnie and Billie Bushytail, the squirrel boys!"

"What has happened?" asked the hen child.

"They seem to have dropped a bag of sugar, and spilled it all over the woodland path," answered the bunny, as he and Arabella stepped out from behind a bush.

"Johnnie spilled it—I didn't!" chattered Billie Bushytail. "He was carrying the bag of sugar from the store. I didn't drop it!"

"Well, you jiggled my paw, and made me drop it!" chattered Johnnie. "It's as much your fault as mine, Billy Bushytail!"   The squirrel boys looked sad.

"Never mind!" cackled Arabella. "I will pick up the sugar for you! With my yellow beak, just made for picking things up, I can save every grain of sugar for you!"

"Oh, how jolly!" chattered Billie. "Now Mother won't scold us!"

"It's the best thing in the world to have happened," said Uncle Wiggily. "Arabella, I'm glad I have you with me this morning. Now, squirrel boys, brush the spilled sugar up in a heap with your bushy tails. In that way you can scoop up some in your paws. The other scattered grains Arabella can best pick up in her beak."

"We'll do that!" chattered Johnnie and Billie.

Using their tails for brushes they made a pile of as much of the spilled sugar as they could.

"What shall we put it in?" asked Billie. "The bag is busted."

"You should say 'burst,' not 'busted,' Billie," corrected Uncle Wiggily, gently. "As for a bag, I'll hop on to the store and get one. I have to go to the store for Nurse Jane anyhow, to get something she wanted. I'll do that instead of borrowing it from Mrs. Kinkytail, the monkey lady. It will be better that way. And when I'm at the store I'll get an extra bag."

So Uncle Wiggily hopped off through the woods, while Arabella, with her wings, helped the squirrel boys brush up the spilled sugar into a heap.

"There's no use picking it up until we have something to put it in," said Arabella.

They had it as nicely swept up as could be, when the bunny gentleman came hopping back with a bag, and also something else—something Nurse Jane had told him to bring her.

"Now, Arabella," cried the bunny gentleman "after the squirrel boys scoop up all the sugar they can in their paws, you may pick up the scattered grains in your beak and then——"

"Yes, but before then something else is going to happen!" cried a savage voice from behind a tree, and, as the hen girl looked, ALL OF A SUDDEN, a Long-necked Giraffe ran after the bunny, crying, "I want you!"

Quick as a wink, Uncle Wiggily picked up the bag of sugar and threw it right at the Giraffe who caught it in his mouth.

"I'm glad a giraffe loves sugar," said Uncle Wiggily.

"Now the bad animal can't hurt any of us," chuckled Uncle Wiggily, as he went back to where Arabella, Johnnie and Billie were standing beside the heap of spilled sugar. "It's lucky I happened to go to the store for the paper bag, else I wouldn't have gotten what Nurse Jane asked me not to forget. But everything is all right now. Pick up the sugar!"

Then with their paws the squirrel boys scooped up as much of the sweet stuff as they could, putting it in the new bag. And Arabella picked up the scattered grains in her beak, so that not one was lost.

"Mother's going to make a cake with this sugar," chattered Billie as they all went home together.

"And she'll give us each a slice," added Johnnie; which Mrs. Bushytail did, not forgetting Arabella and Mr. Long-ears.

Thus everything happened for the best, you see, and if the frying pan doesn't go to sleep in the cat's cradle, and forget to awaken in time for breakfast, I'll tell you next about Uncle Wiggily and Neddie Stubtail.

STORY IX

UNCLE WIGGILY AND NEDDIE STUBTAIL

ONE morning Mr. Stubtail, the gentleman bear who was the father of Neddie and Beckie Stubtail, the two children bears, did not come down stairs to breakfast. Mrs. Stubtail had cooked him some gooseberry honey fritters, and they smelled so deliciously throughout the bear cave that Neddie and Beckie could scarcely wait to eat their share.

"Neddie, I wish you'd see what's keeping your father," said Mrs. Stubtail. "He was never late for breakfast before—at least not since he had a boil on the end of his nose. Go see what's the matter, Neddie my dear!"

Up stairs in the cave house clambered the boy bear, but he soon came shuffling down again.

"Is anything the matter?" asked Mrs. Stubtail, anxiously.

"Yes, daddy says he isn't feeling well this morning, and he doesn't want any breakfast, thank you," reported Neddie.

"Oh, is your father ill!" cried the mother bear. "I must send for Dr. Possum right away! Children, eat your breakfasts, and then go along to school, Beckie."

"Isn't Neddie coming to school with me?" asked the little girl bear.

"Not until he goes for Dr. Possum," answered her mother. "I'd telephone for him, but our telephone is out of order. However, Neddie can telephone from one of the neighbors' houses. He may be a little bit late at school, Beckie, so you please tell the lady mouse teacher."

"I will," promised Neddie's sister.

The gooseberry honey fritters did not taste quite so good to the children bears, now that they knew their daddy was ill. But they managed to eat their breakfasts, and then, when Beckie went to school, Neddie ran over to the house of Mrs. Wibblewobble, the duck lady, and telephoned for Dr. Possum.

"Oh, is your father ill?" quacked Mrs. Wibblewobble, when she heard the news. "I'm so sorry! Here is a bit of water-cress salad for him."

"Thank you," rumbled Neddie in a deep, bass voice—not that he was cross when he rumbled, but that is the way all bears speak, you know.

Dr. Possum came to the Stubtail cave so quickly, after he was telephoned to, that he arrived before Neddie had time to gather up his books and amble on to school.

"Better have Neddie wait a little longer," said Dr. Possum to Mrs. Stubtail. "After I find out what is the matter with your husband, I may want him to have something special to eat, and Neddie can get it."

Neddie was glad enough to wait, you may be sure. It wasn't that he didn't like to go to school—mercy no! But he wanted to do all he could for his father, you see; of course!

After a while Dr. Possum came down stairs with Mrs. Stubtail.

"Is my father going to die?" asked Neddie, anxiously.

"Bless your short little tail—no!" laughed Dr. Possum. "He has just a little touch of indispepsia, and what he needs

is some wild bee honey. Do you think you could find some
wild honey in the woods, Neddie? I'm sure the bees will give
you some for your father."

"I'll go look for a bee tree," offered the boy bear.

"Get Uncle Wiggily to go with you," suggested Dr. Possum. "He was telling me, only the other day, how he helped
a bee out of a flower where the honey-buzzer had been closed
in by mistake. If the rabbit uncle knows where this bee lives,
you can easily get some honey for your father."

"I'll hurry right over to Uncle Wiggily's bungalow," rumbled Neddie. "I don't have to go to school; do I?" he asked,
to make sure.

"Not until this afternoon, if at all," his mother answered,
patting his shaggy head with her big, soft paw, and she was
careful not to let her claws scratch Neddie as she patted him.

Off through the woods ambled the boy bear, swaying from
side to side like a sailor on the deck of his ship, for that is
the way bears walk, you know; being rather fat and clumsy,
though at times they can run quite swiftly.

Neddie saw Uncle Wiggily hopping down the front steps
of his hollow stump bungalow.

"I'm just in time!" thought the boy bear. "I'll hurry and
catch him before he goes adventuring."

"What ho, Neddie! Whither away?" called the bunny
gentleman, for he had just been reading a book about the
brave knights of the olden days, when people talked like that.

"I want to find some wild bee honey for my father who is
ill," explained Neddie, "and I thought maybe you could help
me."

"Of course I can!" cried jolly Uncle Wiggily. "I'm sorry to hear your father is ill, but some wild honey will soon make him feel better. You bears are very fond of sweet things, I know."

"Yes, I love honey!" spoke Neddie, and his mouth fairly "watered" for it, as the saying is. "But I'm not going to eat any, no matter how much we find!" he quickly said. "It's all for my father!"

"That's right!" agreed Uncle Wiggily, giving his pink nose a gladsome and happy twinkle. "Now we'll start out, Neddie. I was wondering what I was to do for an adventure to-day, and along you come just in time."

"I haven't any adventure," said Neddie. "I'm sorry, but I haven't any!"

"No, but when I go with you to hunt for wild bee honey that may lead us to an adventure!" chuckled the rabbit uncle. "What ho, my Merrie Men! Lead on!" he cried, still thinking of the knighthood book he had been reading.

"Just a moment, before you do any of that 'what hoeing' or 'raking', either!" called Nurse Jane from the window. Miss Fuzzy Wuzzy had what may be called a prosaic mind. "Just a moment, Wiggy!" she said.

"Yes, Nurse Jane, what is it?" patiently asked the bunny.

"Don't forget to stop at the store while you're adventuring," went on the muskrat lady housekeeper. "You know I told you I needed something!"

"I'll get it," quickly promised the bunny. "And now, Neddie, once again! What ho!"

In this jolly, merry fashion Uncle Wiggily and the boy

bear traveled together over the fields and through the woods, looking for a hollow honey tree, since most wild bees build their nests in such places.

"Hark!" Uncle Wiggily would say every now and then.

"What for—hark?" asked Neddie, curious like.

"I want to listen for perhaps I may hear a bee buzzing," answered the bunny.

Then the two friends would stop in the woods and listen. They would hear the sound of the wind blowing through the trees. They would hear the distant singing of the robin or song sparrow, but no buzzing of bees did they hear.

Once, just as Neddie stopped to pick a red flower, which he thought would cheer up his mother, who, he knew was sad because his father was ill, once Neddie heard a sound that caused him to call to Uncle Wiggily:

"Hark!"

"What is it now?" asked the bunny uncle. "Do you, at last, hear the buzzing of a bee, which tells us we are near some wild honey?"

"No, Uncle Wiggily, I don't exactly hear a bee," answered Neddie. "But I think it must be a little kitten lost out here in the woods all alone. Perhaps it is a new baby kitten sister of Tommie, Joie or Kittie Kat."

"Perhaps," agreed Uncle Wiggily. "Keep very quiet now, and we'll both listen."

It was very still and quiet in the woods just then. And, all of a sudden, to the ears of Uncle Wiggily and the boy bear came the sound of:

"Mew! Mew! Mew!"

"It is a kitten!" exclaimed the bunny.

"I thought it was," rumbled Neddie in his deep, bass voice. "We must find it and take care of it, Uncle Wiggily. We can still do that and have time to get honey for my father."

"I think so—yes," agreed Uncle Wiggily. "Now listen again until we make sure where the sound came from."

Once more the bunny gentleman and the boy bear strained their ears to listen. Again came the sound:

"Mew! Mew! Mew!"

"It's away up in that tall tree!" cried Neddie, pointing with his paw toward a towering cedar.

"That's where it seemed to sound," spoke the bunny. "But how did a poor little lost kitten ever get away up in that tree."

"Some dog might have chased it," suggested Neddie. "No good dog, like Old Percival, or Jackie or Peetie Bow Wow; but some bad dog."

"Perhaps," agreed Uncle Wiggily. "Well, no matter how the poor little pussy got up the tree, we must get it down. And I am glad you are with me, Neddie, for you are such a good climber of trees."

"Yes, I can scramble up pretty well," said Neddie modestly, for it is not right to be proud, you know. "I'll just stick my claws in the bark, shinny up the tree and bring down the kitten," said the bear.

Just then a bird flew out of the tree.

"Oh, Mr. Bird, did you see a poor little lost pussy in that tree?" asked Uncle Wiggily.

"Ha! Ha!" laughed the bird. "I am sorry if I fooled you, Uncle Wiggily, for really I didn't mean to. But I am what is called a cat-bird, and one of my songs is 'Mew! Mew! Mew!' It must have been that which you heard. There is no lost kitten in the tree, I'm sure."

The bunny
jumped back

The boy bear was beginning to fear that they never would get any wild bee honey for his father when, all of a sudden, as Uncle Wiggily leaned over to smell the perfume of a red flower, the bunny jumped back with a little howl.

"What's the matter?" asked Neddie.

"That flower bit me on the end of my pink, twinkling nose!" answered Mr. Longears, holding his paw to his face.

"No, indeed, I didn't bite you!" whispered the flower, nodding her head in the summer breeze.

"Well, something nipped my nose!" said the bunny.

"Oh, I guess I did that," buzzed a gentle voice, "and I'm very sorry I did it, Uncle Wiggily. I'm a bee—the same one whom you once before helped out of a closed-up flower. I didn't mean to hurt you, Uncle Wiggily. But when you leaned over so suddenly, to smell the flower where I was gathering honey, I thought it was a bad animal after me, and I stung you a little bit before I saw who it was."

"Oh, that's all right," said the bunny with a smile. "Don't worry about me. I'll put a little wet mud on the end of my nose, and that will stop the pain."

While Uncle Wiggily was doing this, Neddie watched the bee flit from flower to flower, gathering sweet juices from the blossoms. Then the boy bear asked:

"Could you please give me and Uncle Wiggily a little wild honey for my father, who is ill?"

"Of course I could!" buzzed the bee. "Come to the hollow tree with me and I'll give you as much honey as you need."

"Yes, go along with the bee, Neddie," spoke Mr. Longears. "And while you are getting the honey I'll hop to the store and buy what Nurse Jane asked me to. After that I'll wait here for you to come back with the honey."

So Neddie followed the bee through the woods to get the sweet stuff, the honey-buzzer flying slowly along so the boy bear could easily keep up. Uncle Wiggily hopped to the store, bought what Nurse Jane had told him to, and, coming back to where he had parted from Neddie and the bee, the bunny gentleman sat down on a log to wait until they came back.

It was so warm and quiet in the woods that, almost before he knew it, Uncle Wiggily had fallen asleep.

"Ah ha! Now's my chance to get him!" whispered a savage voice in the bushes. "Now I'll nibble his ears!"

Just then Neddie came back with a birch bark box of wild honey which the kind bee had given him. The bear boy saw what was going to happen.

"Wake up, Uncle Wiggily! Wake up!" howled Neddie. "Oh, wake up!"

Uncle Wiggily opened his eyes, he started to run, but, ALL OF A SUDDEN, a Grinning Gorilla leaped out from behind a rock and raced for Uncle Wiggily, crying, "Wait for me!"

Uncle Wiggily had a big coconut, which he had bought for Nurse Jane, and he threw it in front of the Gorilla, who stopped to eat it.

"How fond he is of coconut," said the bunny. "While he's eating it I can get away."

———

"You're saved, Uncle Wiggily!   You're saved!" cried Neddie, as he and the bunny hurried along after the bad animal had run away.

"Yes, once more I am all right!" chuckled Mr. Longears. "And now we must hasten home with the honey for your father, Neddie. Sometimes," went on the rabbit gentleman, "sometimes I begin to get tired of bringing Nurse Jane so many things from the store, or from the animal ladies who have borrowed them from my muskrat lady housekeeper. But, every time I get into danger, something of Nurse Jane's always helps me out."

"I say that's a good thing!" rumbled Neddie.

"I say so myself!" chuckled the bunny. "Very good indeed!"

The wild honey soon made Mr. Stubtail well; and if the milk pitcher doesn't try to go swimming in the bottle of ink and gets its nose all black, I'll tell you next about Uncle Wiggily and Bully No-Tail.

STORY X

UNCLE WIGGILY AND BULLY NO-TAIL

"Where are you going today, Uncle Wiggily?" asked Nurse Jane Fuzzy Wuzzy one morning, as the rabbit gentleman was hopping away from his hollow stump bungalow.

"Where am I going? Why, I am going to school, Nurse Jane," answered Mr. Longears, with a cheerful twinkle of his pink nose.

"To *school?*" cried the muskrat lady housekeeper. "I thought your schooldays were over long ago! But then I forget—you never will grow up, and I like you all the better for it, Wiggy! I think I shall call you—Peter Pan!"

"Why Peter Pan?" asked the bunny.

"Don't you remember? He was a boy who never, never would grow up! You remind me of him very much. So hop along to school and——"

"Oh, I'm not really going to school to study!" laughed the bunny. "Not but what I couldn't learn many things more," he said, "for all of us can learn something new every day, no matter how long we study. But I am just going to school to visit the lady mouse teacher, and hear some of the animal boys and girls recite.

"You see this is a sort of jolly, festive, holiday occasion at the hollow stump school. There are to be special exercises and Miss Lady Mouse asked me to come and sit on the platform with her." Uncle Wiggily looked rather proud.

92

"Oh, well, hop along then!" laughed Nurse Jane. "And, while you are about it you may as well stop at the twelve and thirteen cent store and get something I need. I told you at breakfast time. Do you remember?"

"Oh, yes, I won't forget!" promised the bunny. "I'll go to the store for you and get what you want. And maybe I'll have an adventure with it—who knows?"

"Not I!" answered Nurse Jane with a smile. "I'm sure I don't know. But as you have an adventure nearly every day, I suppose you'll find one now. Good luck to you!"

"Thank you!" cried Uncle Wiggily as he hopped away. "Thank you!"

It was not far from his bungalow to the big hollow stump where the lady mouse teacher heard the lessons of the animal boys and girls. On the way the bunny gentleman looked on each side of the path, hoping he might find an adventure, but there seemed to be none.

"Ah, well, perhaps I shall find one after school," said the bunny, hopeful like.

All the little boy and girl animals were in their seats when Uncle Wiggily reached the school and started to hop inside. There they sat, from Sammie and Susie Littletail, the rabbits, to Woodie and Waddie Chuck, the groundhog boys.

"Oh, here comes Uncle Wiggily!" squeaked the lady mouse, as she saw the bunny rabbit entering. "Show how pleased you are to see him, children!"

"Good morning, Uncle Wiggily!" cried the animal boys and girls. Those who had paws clapped them and those who had tails wagged them while those who had wings flapped them—thus making joyful noises to greet the bunny uncle.

"Thank you very much for your gladsome welcome!" laughed Mr. Longears, as he took his seat on the platform near the lady mouse teacher. "And now let me hear you boys and girls recite. I want, most of all, to hear that little verse about: 'Once a cheese was baited, with a piece of trap.' Who will recite that?"

To the surprise of Uncle Wiggily, all the children, and even the lady mouse teacher, burst out laughing.

"Why, what is the matter?" asked the rabbit gentleman, his pink nose almost twinkling upside down in his astonishment.

"You said it backwards, that is all," gently explained Miss Mouse. "It should be 'Once a mouse was cheesing with——' "

"Ha! Ha!" laughed the animal boys and girls. "Teacher has it wrong too! Ha! Ha!"

"Yes, so I have!" said Miss Mouse with a confused little smile. "I am so excited, having Uncle Wiggily come to visit us, that I don't know quite what I am saying. But we all remember the little verse he wants to have recited, so I will call on Kittie Kat."

Kittie Kat came up on the platform and very nicely and correctly she recited the little poem about the mouse, the trap and the piece of cheese.

"Fine! Fine! Very well done, indeed!" cried Uncle Wiggily, clapping his paws. "What is next, Miss Mouse?"

"Well," answered the teacher of the hollow stump school, "I next wanted to have the kindergarten class sing a flower-song for you, but we haven't any flowers, and so I'm afraid they can't sing."

The kindergarten class of the littlest boy and girl animals, including Baby Bunty and Friskie, the woodchuck girl, as well as Squeakie Squealer, the tiny pig, looked so sad and unhappy that Uncle Wiggily exclaimed:

The kindergarten class looked so sad

"What! No flowers?"

"No," sorrowfully answered the lady mouse. "I told some of the older animal boys and girls to bring flowers so the babies might do their song this morning, but no one brought a blossom."

"That's too bad!" said the bunny.

"Please, teacher, we all forgot!" croaked Bully No-Tail, the frog boy. "But if you'll let me go out now, I can soon hop to a place where some lovely flowers grow. I'll pick them and bring them back here, and the kindergarten class can have their blossom-drill and sing. Please let me go get some flowers!"

"And let me go with him!" begged Bawly, who was Bully's brother.

A little smile came over the face of the lady mouse teacher as she said:

"It is very kind of you, Bully No-Tail, to offer to go for flowers for the school. And it is very kind of you, Bawly, to want to go with your brother. But I am afraid, if I send you two boys, you'll get to playing ball, or leap-frog, or tag or something like that, and you will forget to come back."

"Oh, no we won't—we promise!" croaked Bully and Bawly together. "Please let us hop after flowers!"

"Shall I let them go, Uncle Wiggily?" asked the lady mouse, frisking her tail sideways.

The bunny gentleman gently twinkled his pink nose.

"Ahem!" he exclaimed, after thinking a moment. "The best plan will be," he said in his jolly manner, "for me to go with Bully after the flowers. In that way there will be no playing leap-frog, and we will come back, as soon as we can, with blossoms for the kindergartners."

"Oh that will be lovely!" said the lady mouse teacher, clapping her paws. "Isn't that fine, boys and girls?"

"Yes! Yes!" shouted all the animal children. "Let Uncle Wiggily and Bully go for the flowers!"

So it turned out that way. Down the school yard path hopped the bunny gentleman and the frog boy, while the pupils awaiting their return, sang a song about the chalk and blackboard running up and down, to chase the feather duster all around the town.

"That was a very pretty song," said the lady mouse teacher, when the children had finished. "Now would you like to sing another?"

"Oh yes, Teacher!"

"Please, yes, Lady Mouse!"

"The song about the Chocolate Cake!"

"No, the one about the Big Balloon!"

So many of the animal boys and girls were trying to speak at once, fluttering their paws or their wings, or snapping their tails, all trying to get the teacher's attention, that the lady mouse held her paws over her ears and closed her eyes.

"Please, children! Please be quiet!" she begged. "We will sing the Balloon Song!"

"Oh, goodie!" cried the girls. Perhaps the boys would rather have sung about the Chocolate Cake, as they were so often hungry. But after the lady mouse had decided they were to sing about the Balloon everyone was happy. So they sang the song, which goes something like this:

> Once there was a Big Balloon
> It floated up so high.
> It sailed away in August
> And came back in July

Below it hung a basket
And in it were some eggs.
All white and round they were at first,
But, later, they had legs.

And how was this, you ask me.
Ah ha! The plot doth thicken!
But all I need to tell you is—
That each egg held a chicken!

"Please could we sing another song, Teacher?" asked Baby Bunty, when the balloon melody was ended.

"Not now, my dear. We must study our lessons," answered the lady mouse. "Soon Uncle Wiggily and Bully will come back with flowers; then we may sing again."

Uncle Wiggily and the frog boy had much jolly fun going through the fields together, and the only accident that happened was once, when Uncle Wiggily tried to jump over a puddle of water, he slipped.

"Oh, look out!" croaked Bully, as one of the bunny's legs made a big splash.

"Too late! I'm already in!" laughed Uncle Wiggily. "Come over here and help me, Bully, or I may topple in altogether, and I don't want a bath just now!"

Bully hurried over to the puddle, and pulled Uncle Wiggily safely up on the bank. The bunny shook the water off his wet leg, and on they went together again.

"Over this way, Uncle Wiggily!" called Bully, as they reached the edge of the woods. "The flowers I spoke of grow in here."

"But this is a swamp, full of old, dead trees, ferns, puddles of mucky water and the like," said Mr. Longears. "It's a dismal swamp!"

"I know it is a swamp," croaked Bully. "But, all the same, some very beautiful flowers grow here."

Uncle Wiggily shook his head doubtful like.

"I think you are making a mistake, Bully," he said. "You should look for flowers on the hill where the sun shines."

"You wait!" croaked Bully. "I'll soon show you some lovely, white flowers that smell most wonderfully, even if they do grow in a black, mucky swamp!"

By this time they had reached the swamp. It was not a very pleasant place, and as Uncle Wiggily looked at the big puddles of black, muddy water he sadly exclaimed:

"No pretty flowers grow here!"

"Oh yes they do—look!" suddenly cried Bully, and with one paw he pointed to a beautiful, perfumed water lily, lying flat on the surface of the black, muddy water. In the centre of the unfolded white petals was a patch of yellow, as though a golden sunbeam had nestled there to sleep.

"Oh, how beautiful!" cried Uncle Wiggily. "I must pick some!"

"No, please, you must let me pick them," croaked Bully. "I am a frog, and I can jump in, swim under water and easily bite off the long stem of the water lily. Its roots are away down in the black mud, but the blossom is white like the snow. I'll get the flowers, Uncle Wiggily. You stay on shore and watch me. You'll sink down in the muck, and get all wet, if you come any farther. Let me flop in."

"Well, all right, and while you are gathering the pond lilies I'll go to the store and get what Nurse Jane wants," said the bunny. "Wait here until I come back!"

"I will," promised Bully as he waded into the black water to gather the beautiful, spicy-perfumed flowers. The frog boy had gathered quite a bouquet of blossoms, and he was thinking how the lady mouse teacher would like them, when he heard Uncle Wiggily coming back. The frog boy looked up and saw something that made him quickly shout:

"Oh, Uncle Wiggily! Look behind you! See what's chasing you! Oh, the bad animal! What can you do to drive him away? Look! Look!"

And then, as Bully looked, ALL OF A SUDDEN, a big Hippopotamus crashed after Uncle Wiggily, crying: "I want to nibble your ears!"

"Oh ho!" laughed the bunny. "This water melon just fits your mouth! Now let's see you nibble!" and he threw the water melon he had bought for Nurse Jane, right at the big Hippopotamus.

"Ha! Ha!" laughed Bully the frog, as he climbed out of the swamp with the bunch of water lilies, after the bad animal had run away. "That was very smart of you, Uncle Wiggily! Very smart and clever!"

"Thank you," panted the bunny gentleman, who was a little out of breath from what had happened. "I'm glad to hear you say so! I think we are safe now, and can go back to school."

"Yes," said Bully. "But wait until I wash some of the mud off my feet. I don't want to dirty the floor. The lady mouse teacher wouldn't like it."

Soon the frog boy and the bunny gentleman were back at the hollow stump school.

"Oh, how lovely!" squeaked the lady mouse teacher as she smelled the spicy odor of the pond lilies. "Now the kindergarten class can sing its flower-song."

"Yes, and then Uncle Wiggily can tell the story of how he got away from the bad animal!" croaked Bully. And the rabbit gentleman did, just as I have told it to you here.

Thus, once more, everything happened for the best, and if the door knob doesn't try to crawl in through the keyhole to go to sleep in the cat's cradle with the gold fish, I'll tell you next about Uncle Wiggily and Nannie Wagtail.

STORY XI

UNCLE WIGGILY AND NANNIE WAGTAIL

"Look who's coming here!" cried Uncle Wiggily one morning as he sat at a window of his hollow stump bungalow looking out. He had just eaten his breakfast, and Nurse Jane was clearing away the dishes. "I do hope she hasn't the Wolf with her!" said the bunny gentleman.

"Goodness me sakes alive and a milk bottle full of soap bubbles!" exclaimed Nurse Jane. "Don't say 'Wolf' to me! Is he really coming? If he is lock the doors and telephone for the Police Dog!"

"Nonsense!" laughed Uncle Wiggily. "I didn't say I *saw* a Wolf coming. I only said I *hoped* she didn't have the Wolf with her!"

"Who?" asked the muskrat lady housekeeper, taking a tight hold of the bread plate, ready to throw it in case some bad animal might try to climb through the window. "Who is coming, Wiggy?"

"Little Red Riding Hood," answered the bunny. "There she comes, with her basket of good things—on the way to see her Grandmother, I suppose, just as it tells about in the story book!"

"Oh—Little Red Riding Hood!" exclaimed Miss Fuzzy Wuzzy. "She is all right. But I didn't know Mother Hubbard or Mother Goose would let her come so far away. Where is she?" The muskrat lady peered from the window.

102

Uncle Wiggily pointed to a tiny figure toddling along, all dressed in bright red. Nurse Jane gave one look and called out:

"That isn't Little Red Riding Hood!"

"No? Who is it then?" asked Mr. Longears.

"Why, it's Nannie Wagtail, the goat girl!" replied Nurse Jane. "She is wearing her new red dress."

"Well, she looks like Little Red Riding Hood, anyhow," spoke the bunny.

"So she does," agreed Nurse Jane.

"And she has a little basket, and maybe it has something good in it," went on Mr. Longears.

"Yes; that's so," admitted Miss Fuzzy Wuzzy.

"And if there isn't something good in the basket you or I could put something in," chuckled the bunny—"a bit of cake or pie."

"Yes," said Nurse Jane. "That could be done," and she smiled at Uncle Wiggily to see him so jolly.

"And," continued Mr. Longears with a queer little twinkle of his pink nose, "if Nannie isn't going to see her Grandmother, she is going to call on Aunt Lettie, the dear old goat lady, which is very much the same thing."

"Well, you might call it that," Nurse Jane said.

"So you see, after all, I wasn't so far wrong in calling Nannie Wagtail by the name Little Red Riding Hood!" laughed the bunny.

"All except the Wolf!" exclaimed the muskrat lady housekeeper.

"Yes, all except the Wolf," agreed Uncle Wiggily, "and I don't want to see him!"

"Nor I!" shuddered Nurse Jane, looking over her shoulder, as if the bad animal might, even then, be creeping up. But he wasn't, I'm glad to tell you.

By this time Nannie, the goat girl, with her red dress, her red bonnet and her little basket, which also happened to be red, had reached the hollow stump bungalow. Nannie looked at the open window and saw Mr. Longears and Nurse Jane watching her.

"Ooo—hoo! Hello, Uncle Wiggily and Nurse Jane!" bleated Nannie, kissing her hoof to her friends in the bungalow.

"Where are you going, Nannie?" asked the bunny gentleman. "Perhaps I'd better go with her," he said, turning to Nurse Jane. "If she is going through the woods, there might happen to be a Wolf or a Fox or a Bear and——"

"Yes, it would be an adventure for you—I can see that!" laughed Nurse Jane, after she had begged Uncle Wiggily's pardon for speaking before he had quite finished.

"Oh, that's all right!" chuckled the bunny. "Yes, it would be an adventure, as you say. I think I'll go with Nannie. Where are you going?" he asked the goat girl.

"Over to my Aunt Lettie's house," Nannie answered. "Aunt Lettie isn't feeling very well and my mother is sending her a little paste pudding with some circus poster sauce sprinkled over the edges."

"Hum!" laughed Uncle Wiggily with another twinkle of his pink nose. "Paste pudding with poster sauce may be all right for goats, but I don't care for it myself. Have we anything in the bungalow to send to Aunt Lettie?" he asked the muskrat lady housekeeper.

"I have a carrot pie," answered Nurse Jane.

"Oh, Aunt Lettie just loves carrot pie!" bleated Nannie. "I'm sure she'd like yours."

"Put it in the basket," said Uncle Wiggily quickly, "and I'll hop along with you, Nannie. I haven't been out yet this morning. I need exercise."

"He's hoping for an adventure too," whispered Nurse Jane to Nannie, as she slipped the carrot pie into the red basket, while Uncle Wiggily was getting ready to go with the little goat girl.

"I like adventures myself!" bleated Nannie. "I hope we have a real jolly, exciting one!"

"Oh, listen to the child!" cried Nurse Jane, holding up her paws in surprise.

Soon Uncle Wiggily and Nannie were hopping over the fields and through the woods. All of a sudden Uncle Wiggily stopped, picked up a little piece of bark, and stuck it in his ear.

"Why are you doing that?" asked Nannie, wonderingly.

"So I won't forget," answered the bunny.

"Forget what?" Nannie wanted to know.

"Forget to bring what Nurse Jane told me to buy at the store," answered the bunny. "She always wants me to bring something or other when I go off adventuring, and sometimes I forget unless I do something to remember. Now when I feel that piece of bark tickling me inside my ear, I'll remember

to stop at the store and get what Nurse Jane wants. Sometimes it's one thing and, again, another."

"I'll help you to remember," kindly offered Nannie.

"Thank you," remarked Uncle Wiggily, and once more they

Nannie stumbled

hopped on. Everything would have been most lovely except,
just when they were almost at Aunt Lettie's house, Nannie
stepped into a hole beside the path, she stumbled, fell and out
of the red basket slid the paste pudding and the carrot pie.

The paste pudding spilled all over the pie, and then the

"My! My! How angry that Bull is at the red cloth!" laughed Mr. Longears.

See page 108.

sticky pie rolled along the path, covering itself with leaves, twigs, dirt, gravel and pine needles!

"Oh, Nannie! Are you hurt?" cried Uncle Wiggily, hurrying to pick up the little goat girl.

"N-n-no—no! I'm not hurt!" bleated Nannie. "But look at the lovely pudding and pie we were taking to Aunt Lettie! Look at 'em! They're spoiled!"

"Yes," agreed Uncle Wiggily, as he picked up the basket, "Aunt Lettie can never eat the pie and pudding, covered with dirt as they are. Hello—look at them, would you!" he cried, as thousands of ants came crawling out of a hole in the ground. "It didn't take you jolly little ants long to smell the good things!" said the bunny.

"No," answered one of the ants. "But we came to help you and Nannie if we might, Uncle Wiggily. You are always helping others and now we want to help you."

"How can you?" asked the bunny, doubtful like. "The pudding and pie are so full of dirt, tiny stones, pine needles and such things, that they never can be picked clean."

"Oh, yes they can!" exclaimed the head ant lady, with a little smile. "We ants are very good at that sort of thing. With our tiny jaw pinchers we can pick out the teeniest, weeniest specks; and make the pudding and pie as clean as ever."

"How wonderful!" bleated Nannie, wiping her tears away with her hoof. "Please help us, little ants."

"Yes, do!" begged the bunny gentleman. "It is very good of you to offer. Clean the pudding and pie if you please, kind ants. I'll go to the store to get what Nurse Jane wanted. By the time I come back, Nannie, the pudding and pie will be fit to eat again.   Then we can put them in the basket and take them to Aunt Lettie."

"All right," said Nannie.   "I'll stay and watch the ants work, and you go to the store."

Uncle Wiggily hopped away to get what Nurse Jane had told him to bring from the fifteen and sixteen cent store.   The busy ants swarmed over the pudding and pie, picking off every tiny bit of dirt, leaves and stones as Nannie watched them.

Soon the little goat girl heard a jolly voice calling:

"Here I come, Nannie.   Now we'll hop along."

"It's Uncle Wiggily coming back," bleated the goat girl to the ants, and just then a most unpleasant voice cried:

"Yes, and I'm coming, too!   Here I am!"

With that there was a rustling in the bushes.   Nannie gave a scream, and as she looked at the bunny gentleman, who was hopping toward her, ALL OF A SUDDEN, a big bull ran after Uncle Wiggily, bellowing: "I'll toss your ears!"

Uncle Wiggily had a big roll of red cloth he had bought for Nurse Jane and he tossed it at the big bull.

"My! My! How angry that bull is at the red cloth!" laughed Mr. Longears.

"How wonderful!" bleated Nannie, when she saw what had happened, and made sure that Uncle Wiggily was no longer in danger from the bad animal. "How smart!"

"Yes, you might call that clever," modestly admitted the bunny. "And now let us see how are the ants coming on with the pudding and pie, Nannie?"

"We have the sticks, stones and dirt all cleaned off," said the ants.

"And very kind of you, I'm sure!" complimented Mr. Long-ears, when the bad creature had gone far, far away. "Now we'll take the good things to Aunt Lettie. She'll be glad to get them, and also to see you, Nannie Red Riding Hood!"

"And we can tell her about the adventure!" bleated the goat girl. "Oh, what fun! We can tell Aunt Lettie all about it!"

"Truly enough, so we can!" chuckled the rabbit gentleman. "But what about giving these ants something for their kind-ness?" he asked.

"Oh, there are enough odd crumbs left over from the pie and pudding where they fell from the basket to give us a fine feast," said one of the ants. "That is all we need."

So everyone was happy except the bad animal, and he didn't deserve to be, I suppose. Anyhow, everything ended in a most jolly fashion. And if the lemon squeezer doesn't pinch the tail of the letter Q and make it turn into a B, to sting the J, I'll tell you next about Uncle Wiggily and Jollie Longtail.

STORY XII

UNCLE WIGGILY AND JOLLIE LONGTAIL

WHEN Uncle Wiggily had hopped down the steps of his hollow stump bungalow one morning, the bunny rabbit gentleman came to a stop at the end of the path, near the front gate, and said to himself:

"Let me see now! Which way shall I go—to the right or to the left?"

He could hardly make up his mind, for it did not really matter much which way he went, as he had nothing special to do that day, except to get something from the store for Nurse Jane, and there was no hurry about that.

"If I turn to the left I may have one sort of adventure," thought the bunny gentleman.

And this, of course, was very true.

"But if I turn to the right," said Mr. Longears, thoughtful like, "I may have something quite different happen to me."

This, also, was very true.

"So," said Uncle Wiggily, " I don't know what to do."

In this, you see, he was like the old Woman who lived in a shoe. Only she had so many children she didn't know what to do.

"I'll just shut my eyes and walk along," thought Uncle Wiggily after a bit. "Whichever way I go it will be all right."

So he started out of the gate with his eyes shut, and, first thing you know, he had bumped into the fence. "Bango!"

"What's the matter with you, Wiggy my dear?" called Nurse Jane from a window upstairs, where she was making the beds. "Can't you see where you're going?"

"Yes," answered the bunny, as he opened his eyes and looked at the fence, "but I don't want to go where I'm seeing! It's a sort of game I'm playing!"

"Oh, you will have your joke!" sniffed the muskrat lady housekeeper. Still, and with all that, she couldn't be angry at Uncle Wiggily. "Only don't forget to go to the store for me before you come back!" she called.

"I'll remember not to forget!" promised Mr. Longears, once more starting off.

Along he hopped a few steps farther, not opening his eyes, and when he did take a peep he found that he had turned to the left.

"So be it!" exclaimed the bunny theatrical like and tragic. "I shall now see what Fate has in store for me!" You know —the way it sometimes reads on the screen in the moving pictures.

So Uncle Wiggily started down the left path through the woods. And I don't mind telling you that if he had gone to the right he would have had quite a different adventure from the one he is going to have.

However, let us see what happens, as they say in story books.

Uncle Wiggily had not hopped very far through the woods before, all of a sudden, he heard a rustling in the bushes. The bunny gentleman was just going to look for a place where he might hide his ears (for he thought some bad animal was about to spring out on him) when, all of a quickness, he heard a laughing voice say:

"Hello, Uncle Wiggily!"

The rabbit looked up and there was Jollie Longtail, the cute mousie boy.

"Oh, Jollie! How you frightened me!" panted Uncle Wiggily, holding one paw to his rapidly beating heart.

"I didn't mean to, I'm sure!" said the mousie boy.

"I know you didn't," spoke the bunny with a smile. "I'll be all right in a moment. Where are you going, Jollie?"

"To the store to get some cheese," answered the mousie boy.

"I'll go with you," offered Uncle Wiggily. "It will be an adventure for me, and I can also get what Nurse Jane wants."

So along to the store hopped Mr. Longears with Jollie. But, as it happened, the old gentleman dog who kept the store was all out of what Nurse Jane wanted Uncle Wiggily to bring her.

"We'll have some in to-morrow," he barked.

"That will do me no good now," said Uncle Wiggily. "I'll have to stop at another shop. But give Jollie his cheese."

"I'll bring it right out," barked the grocery dog.

He went down cellar, and came up with such a large, round cheese, like a small cart wheel, that Uncle Wiggily exclaimed:

"Jollie never can carry that! Oh, dear me! It is much too big!"

"It is rather large," agreed the dog, tickling his right ear, thoughtful like. "Still, it is the only cheese I have left, and if Jollie doesn't take it now I can't tell when he'll get another one.   Cheeses are getting scarce."

"Oh, I'll take it!" squeaked the mousie boy, eagerly. "Mother told me not to come home without a cheese, for we haven't a bit in the house for daddy's supper.   I'll try to take this big one home."

"I'll help you," offered Uncle Wiggily.   "I think between us, we can roll the cheese, Jollie!"

"That will be fun!" laughed the mouse boy.   "Come on! I'm glad I met you, Uncle Wiggily!   My sister, Jillie, wanted to come to the store with me, but it's a good thing she didn't, for she isn't big and strong enough to help me with this large cheese!"

"Yes, it is a good thing Uncle Wiggily is here," agreed the grocery dog.   "Now let's see you roll the cheese home.   I'm sorry I haven't what you want, Mr. Longears."

"Oh, I'll get it at another shop," said the bunny, cheerful like.   "Thank you, just the same!   Now come along, Jollie— let's see how good we are at cheese-rolling!"

Out of the store they rolled the big, round cheese, the grocery dog helping them get it over the door sill.

At first matters went very well, for the path back toward Jollie's home was smooth and level.   But soon the path started to turn down hill and the cheese began rolling faster and faster.

"Look out!" cried Uncle Wiggily, who was helping the mouse boy push the cheese along.   "Look out!   It's going to run away from us!"

And run away the cheese did, down the hill!

"Oh, dear! Oh, dear! What shall we do?" squeaked Jollie, standing on top of the hill and looking down at the runaway cheese going faster and faster.

"Don't cry!" said Uncle Wiggily kindly. "The cheese can't run on like the brook, forever, Jollie. The cheese must come to a stop soon, and then we'll get it!"

Surely enough the cheese stopped rolling at the foot of the hill, and toppled over into a ditch.

"Oh dear me, that's bad luck! That's very bad luck!" exclaimed Uncle Wiggily, as he saw Jollie's cheese roll into the ditch.

"Is it worse luck, Uncle Wiggily, to have the cheese roll into a ditch than into some other place?" asked the mouse boy, for this was the first time anything like this had ever happened to him.

"Worse? I should say so!" cried the rabbit gentleman. "Don't you know, Jollie, that there is always water in a ditch? And there is nothing worse for a cheese than water—that is unless it's snow or ice, and there isn't any of that now, as it is so warm. But I am afraid that cheese is done for, Jollie, my boy!"

"Let us hope not," said the mouse chap. "Perhaps it is a dry ditch."

"Perhaps it is," agreed Uncle Wiggily, with a most delicious twinkle of his pink nose. "I never thought of that! If that is a dry ditch, with all the water run out, we are still in luck."

The mouse boy and the gentleman rabbit hurried on to the ditch at the foot of the hill. To their delight they found there wasn't a drop of water in the place, and the cheese wasn't harmed a bit, but it was rather dusty.   Still that could be brushed off.

By hard work Uncle Wiggily and Jollie managed to roll

"Don't let it slip away from us!"

the cheese out of the dry ditch. They got it back on the road and started it off again.

They came to another hill, and started the cheese down it very carefully and slowly. But alas! Suddenly Jollie's paw slipped, he lost hold of the cheese and down hill it rolled again, tumbling into a big hole.

"Can we ever get it out?" asked Jollie as he and the bunny started hopping down hill.

"Oh, I think so," answered Uncle Wiggily, hopeful like.

And they did, I'm glad to say. But it was hard work. The cheese was a bit dented on one side, but of course that didn't spoil it for eating.

But now there was another trouble! The next hill pointed up instead of down, and Uncle Wiggily and Jollie had to roll the big cheese up the hill.

"Be careful now, Jollie, and don't let it slip away from us!" grunted Uncle Wiggily, as they started pushing the cheese up the slope.

"What will happen if I do?" asked the mouse boy.

"I don't like to think of it," answered the rabbit with a shiver. "Look out!" he cried, for he felt something slipping. "Look out!"

"I can't hold the cheese!" shrieked Jollie. "It's rolling back down the hill!"

And that is just what happened! The cheese was too heavy for the two friends to roll up the hill. It slipped away from them. Back down it slid all by itself.

"Oh, dear!" squealed Jollie. "I'll never get this cheese home!"

"Oh, yes we will," laughed jolly Uncle Wiggily. "We mustn't give up so easily!"

Back the cheese rolled, down the hill and into the ditch

once more. By hard work Uncle Wiggily and little Jollie pushed it out and onto the smooth, level road again. Then Uncle Wiggily and Jollie sat down on the cheese to rest.

At last the bunny arose, gave his pink nose a jolly twinkle and said:

"I know what I'm going to do!"

"What?" asked Jollie.

"I'm going back to the store we passed a little while ago. I'll get what Nurse Jane told me to—which the grocery dog didn't have—and then I'll come back here to you. By that time we'll both be rested, and maybe I can think of a new way to help you take the cheese home."

"I hope so," sighed Jollie. "I certainly hope so!"

Uncle Wiggily was just about to hop away when there came a rustling in the bushes—a sound which the rabbit gentleman always feared, for the Woozie Wolf and the Fuzzy Fox generally made this noise.

"Hark! Listen!" squeaked Jollie

"I am listening," said Uncle Wiggily.

"Ah, something is coming out!" whispered Jollie.

"Right you are," murmured Uncle Wiggily, and he looked around for something with which to fight a bad animal, when all of a sudden, Jollie said:

"Oh, how pretty!"

And out from the bushes fluttered a large, red butterfly, and no bad animal at all.

"Hello, Uncle Wiggily," whispered the butterfly. "You and Jollie are so warm with your hard work that I am going to fan you with my wings."

This the butterfly did, cooling the bunny and mouse boy, and then Uncle Wiggily was ready to hop off to the store and get what Nurse Jane had asked him to bring her.

"You stay here and wait for me, Jollie," said the bunny, as he thanked the fanning butterfly, which soon fluttered on to gather honey from a flower.

The mousie boy remained sitting on the flat, round cheese, while Uncle Wiggily hopped off to the store. Pretty soon the bunny gentleman came hopping back again with what he had bought.

But just before he reached Jollie, there was a loud rustling in the bushes and the mousie boy cried:

"Look out for yourself, Uncle Wiggily! Look out!"

And then, ALL OF A SUDDEN, a Bushy Bear jumped out and caught Uncle Wiggily.

At the store, Uncle Wiggily had bought Nurse Jane a vegetable grater and he rubbed it on the nose of the Bushy Bear who howled, "Wow! Wow! Don't grate all my nose away!"

"Good! Good!" squeaked Jollie, when Uncle Wiggily was finally safe. "Now that you have driven away the bad animal, have you thought of a way to help me get the cheese home?"

"Yes," answered the bunny uncle, "I have. I'm going to ride you home on it, and we'll go around by the longer way where there are no hills."

"How can you ride me home on a cheese?" asked Jollie. "I hope you can, though, for my tail is sore where the cheese ran over it."

"I'll show you!" chuckled the bunny.

He took a pole, made a hole in the cheese, and thrust the long stick through it. On one sticking-out-end of the pole Uncle Wiggily made a little hammock of wild grape vine, and in this hammock he told Jollie to jump. On the other end of the pole, as it stuck through the cheese, the bunny hung a stone, to balance Jollie's weight, like a sea-saw. Then, fastening a long loop of grape vine to the pole, close to either side of the cheese, Uncle Wiggily made some horse reins, and, hitching himself to them, he pulled the cheese along a level road like a wheel, and gave Jollie a fine ride.

"Oh, I wish I had come with you!" squealed Sister Jillie, when she saw her brother coming home riding on the cheese in this style, like a taxicab.

"Get in on the side where the stone is, and I'll give you a little ride, Jillie," laughed the bunny. Then he rode Jollie and Jillie all around, and it didn't hurt the cheese at all.

So everything came out all right, except for the bad animal. And if the doll's new dress doesn't go walking down the street by itself and scare the baby carriage so that it runs away, I'll tell you next about Uncle Wiggily and Jacko Kinkytail.

But of course you must go to bed when the right time comes, and you musn't wiggle too much when you're sitting on Grandma's lap. Else maybe you'll wear a hole in her apron, and fall through. Anyhow, I think it's time, now, for you to go to sleep, to be ready for the next story.

STORY XIII

UNCLE WIGGILY AND JACKO KINKYTAIL

"Did you hear the news, Uncle Wiggily? Did you hear the news?" exclaimed Nurse Jane Fuzzy Wuzzy one day, as she fairly burst into a room of the hollow stump bungalow where Mr. Longears was reading the paper. I say "burst," for the muskrat lady housekeeper was in such a hurry that one of her shoe laces broke right in the middle as she opened the door.

"News? What news?" asked Uncle Wiggily. "I have been reading the paper since breakfast, Nurse Jane, but the only news I find is that carrots will cost a little more next season, and turnips and lettuce will be a bit cheaper, so I suppose we ought to be thankful for this."

"Oh, it isn't that news I mean!" cried Miss Fuzzy Wuzzy. "This is dreadful news! Didn't you hear?"

"Do you mean the bad old Fuzzy Fox has been arrested and will never bother me again?" asked Uncle Wiggily.

"No, I'm sorry to say it isn't that news," spoke the muskrat lady.

"Well, then, do you mean the Skillery Scallery Alligator has gone back down to Florida, and will never chase me any more?" the bunny gentleman wanted to know.

"Indeed I wish that were true, but I'm afraid it isn't,"

sighed Nurse Jane. "The news I mean is that Jacko Kinkytail is lost!" Sadly the muskrat lady sighed.

"Lost! Jacko Kinkytail lost! That monkey boy?" cried
Uncle Wiggily, jumping up in such surprise that his spectacles
nearly fell off the bridge of his pink, twinkling nose. "Don't
tell me you mean Jacko Kinkytail, the monkey!" begged the
bunny.

"That is just the news I came to tell you!" answered Nurse
Jane. "Jacko's mother sent him to the store to get something
for her, as I often send you, and he hasn't come back, and he
hasn't brought what his mother sent him after."

"Of course he couldn't bring it back—whatever it was—
until he came back himself," said Uncle Wiggily. "But this
is too bad—I mean about Jacko being lost! I must go out
and help find him!"

"That's what I thought you'd want to do, so I came to tell
you as soon as I could," spoke the muskrat lady. "Poor
Jacko!"

"Poor Jacko indeed!" murmured the bunny gentleman.
"But cheer up, Nurse Jane. I may find him. And when I
do I'll bring him safely back to his mother. Where's my
hat? Is my pink nose on straight? Where's my red, white
and blue rheumatism crutch? Or never mind that—I haven't
time to bother, and my rheumatism doesn't hurt now. Where's
my handkerchief? Is my pink nose—Oh, I asked that before,
didn't I?"

So saying, and running around excitedly, Uncle Wiggily
finally got ready to leave his hollow stump bungalow to hop
in search of lost Jacko Kinkytail.

Skipping down through the village of Animal Land, to inquire the latest news and find out which way Jacko was going when he was last seen, Uncle Wiggily found the boys and girls, as well as the grown-up friends of the monkey chap, all in a flutter.

"Call out the fire department!" wheezed Grandpa Whackum, the beaver.

"I think the police would be better," bleated Aunt Lettie, the goat lady.

"Why not advertise in the papers?" asked Uncle Booster, the woodchuck. "We could send Jacko a copy of the paper, with the advertisement in, saying he was lost, and when he sees it he could come home!"

"Nonsense!" exclaimed Uncle Wiggily. "If we knew where Jacko was, to send him a newspaper, he wouldn't be lost!"

"Well, that's so," admitted Uncle Booster, who was always trying to help his animal friends, but generally in the wrong way.

"And," went on Uncle Wiggily, "there is no need for Jacko to read in the paper that he is lost—he knows it already, where ever he is."

"Well, that's so, too," admitted Uncle Booster. "I guess I'll have to think up something else."

"What would you advise, Uncle Wiggily?" asked Mr. Whitewash, the polar bear gentleman.

"I'd advise this," answered the bunny. "First we must ask Mrs. Kinkytail which way she sent Jacko to the store, and then we must look in just the other direction."

"Why the other direction?" asked Mrs. Twistytail, the pig

lady, as she tried her green bonnet on backward to see how that style suited her complexion. "Why not look in the same way that Jacko went to the store?"

"Because," answered Uncle Wiggily, "boys never go to the store the shortest way, or the way you think they ought to go. Nearly always they go in the other direction, to play tag, or leap-frog, and they make their way to the store around through the back lots where there's a ball game going on—isn't that so, boys?" asked Uncle Wiggily.

"Yes, sir," answered Johnnie and Billie Bushytail, the squirrels, and Jackie and Peetie Bow Wow, the puppy dog boys.

"There you are!" laughed Uncle Wiggily, and, somehow or other, everyone felt more jolly after hearing him chuckle. "Now the thing to do," went on the rabbit uncle, "is to ask Mrs. Kinkytail which way she sent Jacko, and then to look just the other way for him."

"We'll do that!" cried the boy and girl animals and the grown-up ones also. They were all friends of poor, lost Jacko Kinkytail, the monkey chap.

Mrs. Kinkytail was in tears when they called at the monkey house to ask her, and Jumpo, who was Jacko's brother, was trying to make his mother feel better by telling her the lost chap would soon be home. Mr. Kinkytail was off in the woods searching.

"He went that way to get me something from the store," said Mrs. Kinkytail, between her sobs, and she pointed with her paw toward the trees of the North forest.

"Then we must look South!" said Uncle Wiggily. "Scatter

now, all of you, and search through the South Woods for Jacko. Scatter and we'll soon find him!"

And away they all scattered.

Uncle Wiggily went off by himself down a path all tangled with bramble bushes and briars, and at times the bunny had to stop and gnaw some of the vines apart with his strong teeth so he could make his way.

"I know Nurse Jane would say Jacko never came in this direction, if she were here," murmured Uncle Wiggily to himself, "but she doesn't know boys. They always go the hardest way! Besides, Jacko could swing along through the tree tops, which I can't do. It would be easier for him to do that. He could jump over the brambles, though I can't. I think I shall find him somewhere along here."

Uncle Wiggily knew that Jacko was such a funny little monkey boy that he might be lost, or hiding in almost any place along the way. So the bunny gentleman looked in every hole, crack, corner and queer little bunk he saw, hoping he might see Jacko's tail sticking out, or catch a glimpse of the monkey chap's fuzzy face or paw.

But when Uncle Wiggily had hopped along for nearly a mile this way, and had seen no sign of the missing monkey, the bunny gentleman began to be a bit frightened.

"What can have happened to Jacko?" he asked himself. "Perhaps he is in a smaller hole than I imagine. After this I'll even look down in the holes of ant hills, for Jacko may have squeezed himself down one of these."

At the next ant hill he came to Uncle Wiggily stopped and, putting on his glasses, he peered down the hole long and anx-

iously.   As he was looking, some of the ants came crawling up
the hole.

"I have lost a little monkey boy, or, rather, he has lost himself," said the bunny.   "I know it seems foolish to look for him

Going as fast as he could
go was — Jacko Kinkytail

in an ant hill, but I don't want to miss him.   Have you a little
monkey chap down there?"

"Bless your whiskers, no indeed!" laughed the ants.

"Then I shall have to look elsewhere for Jacko," sighed the
bunny.

But for some time Uncle Wiggily neither saw nor heard

anything of the missing monkey boy. Then, all of a sudden, there was a strange noise in the woods, at the bottom of a little hill, and the bunny gentleman stopped to listen.

"I hope that is Jacko coming, and not some bad animal," thought the bunny.

The noise grew louder. Uncle Wiggily looked up the hill and saw, coming down, a big barrel. The barrel was bounding along, making a booming noise like thunder. And, running along in front of the barrel, going as fast as he could go, in order not to be rolled over, was—Jacko Kinkytail!

"Oh, I've found him! I've found little lost Jacko!" cried Uncle Wiggily. "Oh, rather, he has come to me. Don't run so hard, Jacko!" he called to the monkey boy. "That barrel won't hurt you. It is empty, as I can tell by the sound. Just step to one side and the barrel will roll past you! Don't run so hard! Let the bounding barrel run away by itself!"

"I wish I could!" chattered the monkey boy. "I wish I could! But it won't run! It won't leave me! It keeps chasing me!"

"You don't mean to tell me that empty barrel is chasing you?" cried the bunny as the monkey boy ran nearer.

"Yes, it's fast to my tail!" said poor Jacko. "From the outside I stuck my tail inside through a hole in the barrel. Then a bad animal who was there tied a knot in my tail, and I have to drag the barrel after me where ever I go!"

"You poor boy!" exclaimed Uncle Wiggily. "No wonder you got lost, running through the woods with an empty barrel tied to your tail! And of course you couldn't reach inside to loosen the knot. But stand still, and I'll crawl in the barrel and untie the knot for you. Then you can pull out your tail and I'll take you home. We are all looking for you!"

Jacko stood still and the barrel didn't chase him any more. Then Uncle Wiggily crawled inside and loosened the knot so the monkey boy could pull out his tail, which he did right gladly.

"How did it happen?" asked the bunny.

"Well," answered Jacko, "I went to the store for my mother and got what she asked me to. I was walking along home when I happened to see the barrel with the hole in it. And a voice from within said: 'Stick your tail inside this barrel and you'll get a surprise.' Well I thought maybe it would be a nice surprise, so I stuck my tail through the hole inside the barrel. Then, all at once, some bad animal in the barrel tied a knot in my tail and I couldn't pull it out. I was so frightened that I ran as fast as I could and the barrel rolled after me!"

"What did you do with what your mother sent you to get?" asked the bunny.

"Oh, the bad animal took that away from me—it's inside the barrel. Didn't you see it?" Jacko asked.

"I saw something," replied Uncle Wiggily. "But what bad animal was it that asked you to stick your tail through the hole so he could tie a knot in it? What bad animal?"

"I couldn't see, Uncle Wiggily. He kept himself hidden in the barrel, and maybe he's there yet! Oh dear!"

"No, there's nothing in the barrel but what you got for your mother at the store," said the bunny. "And it's a wonder that didn't bounce out. The bad animal isn't there!"

"Are you sure?" asked Jacko. "You had better look again,
Uncle Wiggily. Sometimes bad animals are very clever and
tricky, and this one may have made himself small and be hiding in one of the cracks of the barrel."

So Uncle Wiggily looked in the barrel, even rattling around
it with a stick and poking his paws in each crack, but he found
nothing.

A good reason, too, for the bad animal, after having played
such an unpleasant trick on Jacko, had slipped out of the barrel, while Uncle Wiggily's back was turned, and was, even
then, hiding in the bushes.

"I'll just sit here until I get a good chance," said the bad
animal to himself, "and then I'll nibble Uncle Wiggily's ears
—that's what I'll do—I'll nibble his ears! Oh, ho! Ha! Ha!"

Wasn't he the unkind, cantankerous old chappie, though?

"Well, did you see anything?" asked Jacko, when Uncle
Wiggily had peered and poked inside the barrel for some time.

"Not a thing, Jacko, my boy," was the answer. "I guess
the worst of your troubles are over."

But the bunny gentleman little knew what was going to
happen.

Jacko, who had been sitting down to rest his poor, pulled
tail stood up, but, as he did so, a cry of pain came from the
monkey boy.

"What's the matter?" quickly asked Mr. Longears. "Is it
the bad fellow?"

"No, I'm glad to say it isn't that," the monkey boy answered. "But, oh such a pain as I have in the end of my tail,
where the knot was tied!"

"I'm sorry for you," spoke the bunny. "If Nurse Jane were only here she would know what to do."

He put some witch hazel on the monkey boy's tail, and soon the pain had nearly all stopped.

"I'm so glad the bad animal isn't there," murmured Jacko, looking at the barrel. "If he were over there, which he isn't, he might——"

"No, but I'm *here!*" quickly cried a savage voice. Uncle Wiggily and Jacko turned around, and the monkey boy shouted:

"Get what's in the barrel, Uncle Wiggily! Get what's in the barrel! That may save you from the bad animal!"

The bunny gentleman just had time to do this and then, ALL OF A SUDDEN, a Fuzzy Fox caught Uncle Wiggily, dragging him by the ears.

Uncle Wiggily opened the package, that he had gotten out of the barrel, and shook it all over the Fuzzy Fox, saying, "Ha! Ha! How do you like red pepper, Mr. Fox?"

"Now is our chance, Jacko! Come on!" whispered Uncle Wiggily, when he saw that he and the monkey boy were safe from the bad animal. "I'll take you home, and you won't be lost any more."

"Oh, I wasn't lost, Uncle Wiggily!" laughed Jacko, who was feeling much better, now that the barrel was no longer tied to his tail.

"You weren't lost?" exclaimed the bunny in surprise. "Why——"

"No, I knew where I was all the while," laughingly answered Jacko. "It was my *house* that was lost. I just didn't know where it was."

"Ho! Ho!" chuckled Uncle Wiggily. "It's the same thing I guess. Well, I know where your house is, so that isn't lost any more."

Then the rabbit gentleman took the monkey boy home, and everyone was glad to see Jacko. So if the piano doesn't try to play tag with the hand organ, and lose its keys so it can't unfasten the lock of the rag doll's hair, I'll tell you next about Uncle Wiggily and Floppy Twistytail.

STORY XIV

UNCLE WIGGILY AND FLOPPY TWISTYTAIL

UNCLE WIGGILY was peacefully sitting on the porch of his hollow stump bungalow one morning, looking at the sunshine and letting it gently tickle his pink, twinkling nose. He was wondering if it might not be time for him to start off on an adventure trip when, all at once, there was a rustling in the honeysuckle vine that grew near the front porch.

"Ha!" exclaimed Uncle Wiggily, sort of excited like. "This sounds like the start of an adventure! Perhaps this is the Woozie Wolf or the Bad Bob Cat come to nibble my ears!"

Uncle Wiggily was getting ready to jump inside the bungalow and lock the door, in case the noise might be made by some bad animal, when, all of a sudden, a little whispering voice asked:

"Is Nurse Jane there?"

"Oh, ho!" exclaimed the bunny uncle. "Are you going to nibble Miss Fuzzy Wuzzy's ears for a change?"

"Nibble Nurse Jane's ears? I guess I wouldn't do such a thing!" cried the voice, in indignant fashion. "I like her too much! But, just now I don't want her to hear what I am saying!"

"Why not, and who are you?" asked the puzzled rabbit uncle, beginning to think this was quite a mysterious and strange happening.

"To answer your last question first," went on the voice, "I am Curly Twistytail, the piggie boy. And the reason I don't want Nurse Jane to hear me is because, if she did, maybe she wouldn't let you come with me."

Out from a clump of honeysuckle vine scrambled Curly Twistytail, the little pig boy, and on the end of his pink, rubbery nose was a little blob of black dirt, which made him look so odd that Uncle Wiggily had to laugh.

"Ho!" grunted Curly, who was given that name because of a funny quirk in the end of his tail, " 'tisn't anything to laugh at!"

"What isn't anything to laugh at?" asked Uncle Wiggily, for he could tell by Curly's voice that something was the matter.

"What happened to my brother Floppy isn't anything to laugh at," grunted Curly.

"Oh, my dear little piggie chap! I wasn't laughing at what happened to Floppy!" exclaimed the bunny, serious like. "I was laughing at the funny little black blob of dirt on the end of your pink, rubbery nose. I know pigs must root in the dirt, so that is all right. I'm not finding any fault. But you do look funny! Here, rub off that blob, or I can't stop laughing! Please do!"

With another grunt, Curly rubbed his nose in the honeysuckle vine and the dirt came off. Then Uncle Wiggily said:

"Excuse me for laughing, Curly, and now tell me what is the matter with your brother Floppy. What has happened to him?"

"He is stuck!" blurted out Curly.

"Stuck!" cried the rabbit uncle.

"Yes," went on Curly. "Stuck! And I came to ask if you would come and help me get him loose, or unstuck!"

"Of course I'll come!" offered Uncle Wiggily. "It will be an adventure for me, and——"

"Not so loud—not so loud, if you please!" grunted Curly, holding one paw up in the air and shaking it at the bunny. "Don't let Nurse Jane hear you or she will not let you come with me! That's why I rooted my way up here so quietly until I could speak to you alone. I don't want Nurse Jane to hear!"

Uncle Wiggily tiptoed down off the porch and walked very softly with Curly down to the end of the garden.

"Perhaps you're right, Curly," said the bunny in a whisper. "There is no need to bother Nurse Jane with this. Poor muskrat lady housekeeper! She has troubles enough of her own! We'll just go off quietly by ourselves—you and I—and when we come back we'll tell her all about it. Then it will be too late for her to make me stay home. But tell me—what happened to your brother Floppy?"

"He's stuck!" said Curly again.

"Where; in the mud by his feet, the way Sammie Littletail was once, with his new boots, or as Lulu Wibblewobble was when she wanted to show me how she could swim?" asked Uncle Wiggily.

"No, Floppy isn't stuck in the mud," grunted Curly. "He's stuck inside a hollow log, and something else is stuck with him!"

"What else is?" the bunny wanted to know. "And for gracious sakes tell me where Floppy is stuck, so I can go and help get him out!"

"That's what I'm going to tell you," said Curly. "Come on, I'll show you where it is, and tell you all about it. But don't make any noise!"

"No, indeed!" agreed Uncle Wiggily, looking anxiously back toward his hollow stump bungalow. "There is no need to worry Nurse Jane until we get back—she might not let me go if she saw me!"

So, crouching down behind the bushes, Uncle Wiggily and Curly walked softly along until they were some distance away from where the bunny gentleman lived in his bungalow.

"Early this morning," explained Curly, as he walked beside the rabbit uncle, "my mother sent Floppy to the store for her. She wanted him to get her something. There is no use asking me what it is, for I don't know. I didn't stop to ask.

"But after a while, when Floppy didn't come back, my mother got anxious and she said I'd better start out and find my brother," added Curly.

"Just the way I started out, and found Jacko Kinkytail when the monkey boy was lost the other day," remarked Uncle Wiggily.

"Yes, just like that," grunted Curly. "Only I knew pretty well where to look for my brother, as we have lots of places where we two play in the woods. I looked in one hiding-out hole after another, but I couldn't find Floppy. Then I grunted as loudly as I could to call him, and all of a sudden, he answered me, and so close to me that I had to jump, I was so surprised."

"Where was he?" asked Uncle Wiggily, eager and puzzled.

"Floppy was inside a hollow log, and I was standing right on top of the log calling to him," explained Curly. "Come over this way, and I'll show you the log."

"Oh, Floppy, what are you doing in there?"

The little piggie boy led Uncle Wiggily through the woods, and soon they came to a green, grassy place where several big trees had fallen down. Some of the trees had rotted away until they were hollow inside, like a large water pipe.

"Floppy's in that hollow log," grunted Curly, pointing to one of the largest of the dead trees on the ground.

"Oh, Floppy, what are you doing in there?" called Uncle Wiggily.

"I'm not doing anything!" grunted Floppy. "I can't do anything! I'm stuck!"

"How did you get in there?" asked the bunny.

"I—I crawled in," squealed Floppy in answer, and his voice sounded as if he might be down in a cellar. "I just crawled in!"

"But why did you do it?" asked Uncle Wiggily.

"Well, I had gone to the store for my mother," replied the piggie boy. "I bought her what she wanted, and on my way home some bad animal chased me. I ran in here to hide, with what I bought for my mother, and here I am yet. Only the log is smaller at one end than it is at the end where I ran in, and I'm stuck fast—like a cork in a bottle!"

"Dear me! That's too bad!" sighed Uncle Wiggily. "What sort of an animal was it that chased you, Floppy?"

"I don't know, Uncle Wiggily. I didn't stop to look," replied the piggie boy. "I just made a dive for the hollow log, crawled in and now I'm stuck! I wiggled and woggled but I couldn't get out. Then I heard Curly calling me, and I answered him, and told him to go get you. I thought maybe you could help me out."

"I think I can, Floppy!" said the bunny gentleman. "Let me think a minute now, to find the best way. Ah, I have it!" he cried. "We'll pull you out with a piece of wild grape vine!"

"How?" asked Curly, curious like.

"Get me a long, strong piece of wild grape vine, and I'll show you," answered the bunny.

Curly found the grape vine, and Uncle Wiggily made a slip knot, cowboy lasso in one end. Then he thrust this loop end of the vine inside the hollow log.

"Tell me, Floppy, when you feel the lasso around one of your legs," called the rabbit gentleman.

"It's around one now!" grunted Floppy, inside the log.

"Now then, Curly, you and I must pull as hard as we can!" shouted the rabbit gentleman. Catching hold of the outside end of the vine, Uncle Wiggily and Curly pulled. Slowly but surely out came Floppy from the hollow log, bringing with him, in his front paws, what his mother had sent him to the store to get.

"Well, Floppy, you had quite an adventure, didn't you?" asked Uncle Wiggily, as the little piggie boy sat down on the grass to rest, after the hard work of having been pulled out of the hollow log.

"Yes, it was a bit exciting," agreed Floppy.

"What did you think about when you were cooped up inside there?" asked his brother Curly, as he looked to see if the kink had come out of his tail. And he was glad to see that it had not.

"Well, I was thinking and wondering what mother would have for supper to-night," grunted Floppy, "and I was hoping, if it was turnip shortcake, with strawberry filling down the middle, that some of it would be saved for me."

Uncle Wiggily was thinking it was about time to start back home, to tell Mrs. Twistytail that the lost piggie chap was found when, all of a sudden, down in the grass a sad little voice said:

"Oh dear, I never have any good times!"

"Bless my pink nose—who's that?" exclaimed Uncle Wiggily, almost stepping on his tall hat in his excitement. "And what's the matter?" asked the bunny.

"Matter enough—I guess you wouldn't be happy if you never had a swing in all your life!" the voice went on.

It was such a cute little voice that they all knew it could not be that of any bad animal, and, looking more closely Uncle Wiggily and the piggie boys saw a ragged little field mouse girl.

"I never had a swing in all my life," she said. "And when I hear others talking about being loved and having good times it—it just makes me all squidgie-widgie like," she sighed.

"You poor little mouse girl! You shall have a swing right now!" said Uncle Wiggily. With the grapevine that had been used to pull Floppy from the log, and with the help of the piggie boys, the bunny made a swing for the field mouse girl.

Curly and Floppy took turns swinging her until it was time for her to go home.

"I'll give you one last high swing!" cried Floppy, and as he pushed the field mouse girl his paws slipped and he fell into a patch of bramble bushes!

"Ha, we must pull you out again!" laughed Uncle Wiggily, and they did this.

"I'd like to know what bad animal chased you in that log!"

said Uncle Wiggily, when the piggie boy was safely out, a little ruffled but not hurt. "I'd like to know who it was!"

"Would you? Then look! I'm the chap who did the chasing!" howled a most unpleasant voice.

Uncle Wiggily and the piggie boys jumped to one side, but it was too late.

"Oh, see what's coming!" squealed Curly. "Look!"

"Here, Uncle Wiggily! Take this!" grunted Floppy, handing the bunny what the piggie boy had bought at the store for his mother. "This may help you!"

Uncle Wiggily just had time to grasp it in his paw, when there was a loud rumble, and again a voice cried:

"I'm the chap who chased Floppy in the log!"

And then, ALL OF A SUDDEN, a Wild Boar, with gleaming tusks, sprang out to get the rabbit uncle.

Uncle Wiggily threw what the piggie boy had bought at the store for his mother and it went right over the head of the Wild Boar.

"Now you can't hurt anyone!" chuckled Uncle Wiggily. "You're muzzled."

"Is everything all right now?" grunted Floppy, when they were safe from the bad animal, who soon ran away, and Uncle Wiggily's ears weren't even so much as snibbled, not to say nibbled.

"Yes, we're all right now," squealed Curly.

"But don't ever again get stuck in a hollow log!" said the bunny gentleman to the piggie boy.

"No'm—I mean no, sir, I won't!" promised Floppy, and he never did. But of course it wasn't altogether his fault; was it? He couldn't help it because a bad animal ran after him; could he?

And now, if the front door mat doesn't chase the milkman around the clothes post and make him churn the cream into sour milk, I'll tell you next about Uncle Wiggily and Dottie Flufftail.

STORY XV

UNCLE WIGGILY AND DOTTIE FLUFFTAIL

"WAIT a moment, Uncle Wiggily! Wait a moment!" called Nurse Jane Fuzzy Wuzzy one morning.

The bunny rabbit gentleman was just hopping down off the steps of his hollow stump bungalow to go adventuring.

"What's the matter now?" asked Mr. Longears, coming to a stop and turning around with a twist of his neck to look at his back. "Is there a raveling, or a bit of woozie-wazzie stuff on my coat?"

"Oh, no, nothing like that!" laughed the muskrat lady housekeeper. "You look as neat as you always do. But I want you to get something for me at the store!"

"Hum! What is it now?" asked the bunny.

"Oh, nothing very much," answered Miss Fuzzy Wuzzy. "It's just something I happen to need. Here, lest you forget, I have written down what I want on this piece of peppermint candy. When you eat the candy you'll remember not to forget what I want."

"I'll be sure to get it," promised the bunny, slipping the round flat peppermint candy in his pocket. "And now, Nurse Jane, if that is all, I'll go adventuring."

"Yes, that is all," the muskrat lady told the bunny. "And I wish you joy and good luck with your adventure!"

142

"Thank you!" responded the bunny, with a low and polite bow. Uncle Wiggily always was polite.

"And may you safely escape from any bad animal that tries to get you!" went on Nurse Jane.

"Thank you again!" laughed the bunny, bowing lower than the first time.

Then he hopped away, over the fields and through the woods, now and then putting his paw in his pocket to make sure he had not lost the peppermint candy that Nurse Jane had given him, with the name of something she needed from the store written on the sweet, spicy wafer.

"I wonder what sort of adventure I shall have this day?" mused Uncle Wiggily as he hopped on and on and on. "Maybe one with a Fox, or perhaps one with a Wolf—who knows?"

Just then Uncle Wiggily's pink nose began to twinkle, and he stopped suddenly beneath a greenwood tree.

"I feel just like singing!" said the bunny. "Yes, I feel a song coming on! I shall stop here and trill a little verse of melody before I go a hop farther!"

Then the bunny lifted his voice, and after a few tra-la-las he chanted this:

> "Off to the woods adventuring,
>   Adventuring I go!
>   I sometimes hop along quite fast,
>   And then, again, quite slow.
> "But whether slow or whether fast,
>   I always gladly sing.
>   For it is very jolly, boys,
>   To go adventuring!"

Uncle Wiggily twinkled his pink nose once more and said, but not singing this time:

"There! I feel much better!"

"I'm glad you do, and I wish I did!" suddenly chirped a sad

"Off to the woods adventuring"

voice in a bush, not far from where the bunny had stopped to trill his summer carol. "Oh, how sad I am!"

"Who are you, and what is the matter?" asked Mr. Longears, for he could tell by the voice that it was none of the bad animals.

"Oh, I'm a poor little bluebird," was the answer. "Last night it rained, and the big drops came down so hard that they washed away my nest, and my little birds are scattered here on the ground! They are such little birds they have hardly any feathers yet, and I dare not leave them uncovered by my wings long enough to build a new nest!"

"Oh my! That is too bad!" cried the bunny. "Let me think what I can do for you. If this was only winter, and I had my fur overcoat I could put your little birds in one of my warm pockets until you had time to build a new nest. But, as it is, these present pockets are not of much use! Let me see now!"

Uncle Wiggily slipped a paw in one pocket and found the peppermint candy Nurse Jane had given him so he would not forget to buy her something at the store.

"Ha! Perhaps if I nibble a bit of peppermint I can think better," said the bunny. "Also it will help me to remember what Nurse Jane wants."

The bunny rabbit gentleman nibbled a bit of the sweet peppermint, and just then, looking up from where the mother bluebird was nestled on the ground over her little ones, Uncle Wiggily saw Dottie Flufftail, the girl lamb, going through the woods.

"Oh, Dottie! Come over here, please!" shouted the bunny.

"Who is calling me, and what do you want?" bleated Dottie, and she prepared to run away in case it might be some bad animal.

"It is I—Uncle Wiggily," answered Mr. Longears. "Here is a poor mother bird and her little ones, washed out of their nest in the rain of last night. She wants a warm place for her teeny-weeny birds to stay until she can build a new nest. Your soft, fluffy, woolly back will be just the place! Will you take care of the little bluebirds, Dottie?"

"Of course I will, right gladly, Uncle Wiggily," joyfully bleated Dottie.

Through the trees she ran until she came to where Uncle Wiggily stood beside the mother bluebird and her little ones, where she was keeping them warm under her wings in the damp grass.

"I'll lift them up on Dottie's back for you, Mother Blue," offered the bunny gentleman. "They can nestle in her warm wool, and Dottie and I will look after them until you build a new nest."

"Oh, how kind you are!" sang the mother bird, her heart now flowing over with happiness. "And if you wouldn't mind taking my little birds home with you, Dottie, and keeping them until I have the new nest built, I'll be a thousand times obliged to you," chirped the bluebird.

"Yes, I'll take your little ones to my house, and keep them safe from harm," promised Dottie. "I was going home, anyhow."

"I'll go with you, and help watch the little birds," offered Uncle Wiggily. "On the way I can get what Nurse Jane wants."

With the little bluebirds nestling down in her warm wool,

Dottie Flufftail walked along through the woods with Uncle Wiggily.

"Good-bye, my little ones, for a short time!" called the mother bird to her birdies. "I'll soon have a new home for you!"

"Peep! Peep!" drowsily answered the little birds, for they were falling asleep in the warm, cozy wool of the lamb girl.

"I'll help you feed them when you get home," said Uncle Wiggily.

Well, he and Dottie were going along most happily together, when, all at once, they heard a sad voice saying:

"Oh, dear! Whatever shall I do? My nest is washed away and I have no place for my little ones!"

"Another bird in trouble from last night's storm!" exclaimed Uncle Wiggily to Dottie. "I wonder what kind this is?"

"I'm a robin," was the answer. "Oh, Uncle Wiggily—for I see it is you—can you help me?" chirped a robin, fluttering on the ground. "The rain washed away my nest and——"

"I know—like the bluebird's!" interrupted the bunny, though he did it most politely. "Well, let me take your little birds, Mrs. Robin. I'll put them in the warm wool of Dottie's back with the tiny bluebirds and there they may stay until you have built a new nest.

"Oh, how kind!" caroled the robin, and when her little birds were on Dottie's warm back the father robin sang a very happy song.

"Good-bye, my little birds!" he sang. "Cheer-up! Cheer-up! Cheer-up! Mother and I will soon have a new nest for you!"

Dottie and Uncle Wiggily were taking the robins and blue-birds to the lamb girl's house, to care for the nestlings, when they heard another sad voice saying:

"Oh, my poor little birds! We no longer have a home since that terrible storm!"

"Ha! More trouble!" cried Uncle Wiggily in his jolly voice. "Who is it this time?"

"I am a song sparrow," was the answer, "and——"

"I know all about it!" laughed the bunny. "You and your little sparrows were washed out of your nest! Well, put your birdies on Dottie's back, and she and I will look after them until you have a new nest built."

"Oh, thank you!" whistled the song sparrow, and then Mr. Sparrow, who was fluttering nearby, sang a most happy song —for you know it is the daddy birds who do most of the sing-ing, the mother birds are too busy.

"My, I'm quite a bird's nest!" bleated Dottie with a laugh as she walked along beside Uncle Wiggily, with the birdies in her wool. "I was going to the store for my mother, but now I guess I had better go home first."

"I'll go to the store for you," offered the bunny. "I have to go for Nurse Jane, anyhow. You eat this peppermint candy, and wait here until I come back with what I have to buy. Sing the birdies to sleep!"

After Uncle Wiggily had hopped away, to go to the store for what he had to buy, Dottie Flufftail, the little lamb girl, remained silent.

"Go on!" peeped some of the little birds. "Aren't you going to do it?"

"Do what?" Dottie wanted to know.

"Aren't you going to sing?" trilled a little robin. "Uncle Wiggily said you'd sing to us."

"Yes, he said you'd sing us to sleep. My mamma always sings me to sleep, and I want to be sung to sleep now," piped one of the song sparrows. "Go on, please sing me to sleep!"

Still Dottie was silent.

"Don't you know any sleepy songs?" asked one of the tiny bluebirds. "My mother — she knows lots of nice little cuddly sleep-songs. But my father, he's a good singer too. He sings better than my mother, but we never tell him so, for fear he'll get proud."

"My father—he's a good singer, too," said a baby robin.

"And so is mine," added a sparrow.

But still Dottie did not sing.

"Peep! Peep! Peep!" went the little birds. "Please sing."

"Well," bleated Dottie at last, "it isn't that I don't know any songs, for I do know three or four. I learned them from the lady mouse teacher in the hollow stump school. But, to tell you the truth, though I know the words I have forgotten the tunes."

"Oh, we don't mind that," said the little birds. "Sing any tune you like as long as the words are funny."

So Dottie hummed this little song:

> "Be quiet, little birdies,
> And nestle in my wool.
> It will keep you nice and warm,
> But, please, you must not pull.

"And if you feel it tickle,
Just stand upon your toes.
And if that does not stop it,
Just stand upon your nose!"

"Ha! Ha! Ha!" laughed all the little birds. "That was a funny song. Please sing another one."

While Dottie sang, the birds nestled in the wool on her back, and pretty soon Uncle Wiggily came hopping back from the store.

"Who is that singing, and waking me up?" quickly cried a harsh voice from the bushes. "Who is singing?" There was a rustling noise and Dottie cried:

"Look behind you, Uncle Wiggily! Jump! Jump!"

The bunny gentleman, returning from the store, jumped, but he was too late. ALL OF A SUDDEN, the Spotted Leopard jumped from the bushes and caught Uncle Wiggily and raised him high in the air.

Quick as a wink Uncle Wiggily squeezed the Spotted Leopard's tail in the lemon squeezer he had bought at the store. It hurt so much that the Spotted Leopard ran away howling.

"I guess he thinks I tried to make lemonade of him," chuckled Uncle Wiggily.

"Oh, how glad I am! How glad I am!" bleated Dottie, when the bad creature was thus driven away, and she was just going to stand up on her hind legs, and clap her front ones, when she happened to remember about the little birds on her back. So she didn't stand up.

"Yes, I'm glad, too," said Uncle Wiggily, when he and the little lamb girl were safely away from the bad animal. "I hope none of the little birds were frightened," whispered the bunny.

And the little bluebirds, robins and song sparrows nestling down in Dottie's warm wool, sleepily chirped:

"Peep! Peep! Peep!"

That meant they weren't a bit frightened, but quite happy, for they were going to sleep.

So Dottie took the little birds with her, and they slept on her back until the new nests were built, and then the father and mother birds had Dottie take the little feathered things to their right homes, where they all lived happily until they grew up and flew away.

So once again the bunny got the best of a bad animal, and if the toy train of cars doesn't run over the parlor rug and make it look like a rag doll going to a picnic, the next story in this book will be about Uncle Wiggily and Woodie Chuck.

STORY XVI

UNCLE WIGGILY AND WOODIE CHUCK

"TAP! Tap! Tap!" sounded a knock on the door of the hollow stump bungalow where Uncle Wiggily Longears lived with Nurse Jane Fuzzy Wuzzy.

The rabbit gentleman was reading his morning newspaper, and the muskrat lady housekeeper had just finished washing the piano and dusting the dishes—or whatever you do after breakfast.

"Tap! Tap! Tap!" sounded again.

"Shall I go to the door?" asked Nurse Jane.

"No, indeed!" exclaimed Uncle Wiggily, quickly. "It might be the Bad Pipsisewah or the Worse Skeezicks, and I wouldn't want them to nibble you!"

"Thank you," spoke Nurse Jane kindly. ˙I don't want to be nibbled if I can help it. But I was just thinking that perhaps it isn't any bad animal at all who is at our door."

"What makes you think that?" asked Uncle Wiggily.

"Because they didn't ring the bell," replied Nurse Jane. "If it was some big, bold animal he would have rung the bell, and not have knocked so timidly."

"Oh, then you think it may be one of the animal boys or girls?" inquired the bunny.

"I am hoping it may be," went on Nurse Jane, as she started for the door.

152

"Wait a minute! I'll take a peep from the side window!" cried Uncle Wiggily. "We'll look before we leap, as the song has it."

The bunny gentleman peered from a window near the door, and what he saw made his pink nose twinkle twice as fast, while a smile spread over his face as he said:

"All right, Woodie! I'll let you in!"

"Oh, one of the Chuck boys," murmured Nurse Jane, and, a moment later Woodie Chuck, a big groundhog or woodchuck boy, came into the hollow stump bungalow.

"Where's your brother Waddie?" asked Nurse Jane.

"Oh, he couldn't come this morning," Woodie answered. "He's helping Uncle Booster dig a little underground house for us to store dried clover in this winter."

"And you are going after chestnuts, I suppose," said Nurse Jane.

"What makes you think Woodie is going after chestnuts?" asked Uncle Wiggily. "Groundhogs don't eat chestnuts, or at least they are not as fond of them as the squirrels are."

"Why I see that Woodie has a bag," went on Nurse Jane, "and I thought he must be going after chestnuts to put in it!"

"No, I am not going after chestnuts," spoke Woodie. "I'm going to the field to get this big bag full of clover to put in the new burrow that Waddie and Uncle Booster are digging. Of course it isn't winter yet," the groundhog boy went on, "but we have to start early gathering the clover. So I'm off to the fields now."

"And you stopped here to get a piece of pie; didn't you?"

asked Uncle Wiggily, winking one eye at Nurse Jane and trying to stop his pink nose from twinkling.

"Yes'm—I mean no'm—Oh, I mean—how did you know I wanted pie?" stammered Woodie, all flustered like.

"Oh, I just guessed it!" chuckled Uncle Wiggily. "All boys like pie. Nurse Jane has some, I guess!"

"No, I'm sorry to say there isn't a bit of pie in the bunga- low!" exclaimed the muskrat lady. "I am just going to bake some pies. I don't suppose you would care for a bit of choco- late cake with carrot frosting on; would you, Woodie?" she asked softly like and unpremeditated.

"Oh, cake! Don't I just love it though!" sighed the ground- hog boy. "But, really, I didn't come to get cake or pie!" he said very earnestly. "Uncle Wiggily made me say that before I thought. I came to ask if Uncle Wiggily would come with me and help me carry back the bag of clover that I am going to gather in the field."

"Surely I'll come with you!" exclaimed the bunny. "You go get Woodie a piece of cake, if you please, Nurse Jane, and I'll find my hat and comb my whiskers. When we come back with the clover maybe you'll have the pie baked," suggested Mr. Longears.

"Yes, I think perhaps, I may," said Nurse Jane with a smile.

The muskrat lady went to the kitchen to get the cake for Woodie, who ate it and thanked Miss Fuzzy Wuzzy very kindly. By this time Uncle Wiggily was ready to hop over the fields and through the woods to the clover meadow with the groundhog boy.

The Pipsisewah ran hard
to catch the bunny gentleman

See page 160.

Woodie carried the empty bag over his shoulder. The bag had long cords fastened to it, and by means of them the opening of the bag could be pulled shut when it was filled with clover.

"And we can drag the bag home along the ground by the same cords," Woodie explained. "That's what they're for; as the bag filled with clover will be too big for us to carry."

"Yes, we'll pull it home as I once pulled home a cheese for Jollie Longtail, the mousie boy," spoke Uncle Wiggily.

It did not take them long to reach the clover field, and there they saw a funny sight. Some grasshoppers were having a race, to see which one could leap the farthest. One big, green chap perched himself on a clover top and cried:

"I can jump farther than anybody in the world! Watch me!"

He perched himself on his hind legs to jump, but, all of a sudden the wind bent the clover top toward the earth. Instead of taking a long far-away jump, the green grasshopper dived right down to the ground and he banged his nose "ker-bunko!"

"Oh, ho! I can jump farther than that!" sang a brown grasshopper. Away he sailed, and as the wind did not blow down his clover top he made a much better jump.

"Ha! Ha!" laughed Uncle Wiggily. "It is best not to say what you are going to do until you do it!"

Then the bunny and the groundhog boy began gathering clover, biting off the stems of the leaves and blossoms and putting them in the big cloth bag with the draw strings, that Woodie had brought with him.

"I'm glad you came with me, Uncle Wiggily," said Woodie, after a while. "I'll get through ever so much more quickly now, and then Waddie and I can play ball."

"And as soon as the bag is filled, and I help you drag it to the store house Uncle Booster is building," said the bunny, "I'm going off and look for an adventure."

But, as it happened, he did not need to go anywhere that day to have something happen. It took place right at his own bungalow.

"Well, I guess the bag is full enough now," said Woodie, as he pushed in the last wisp of clover.

"Yes," agreed the rabbit uncle. "If we stuff it too full we can't pull it."

The cords were drawn tightly around the bag opening, closing it up, and then, taking hold of the long ends of the cords, Uncle Wiggily and Woodie began dragging the bag along. On their way through the meadow the two friends listened to grasshoppers singing jolly little songs; for they were having a sort of picnic, and jumping games were part of the day's sports.

As Uncle Wiggily and Woodie came within a short distance of the hollow stump bungalow, Woodie began to sniff and snuff.

"Don't you smell something, Uncle Wiggily?" asked the groundhog boy.

Then Uncle Wiggily sniffed and smelled.

"Maybe Nurse Jane is baking that pie," suggested Woodie.

"If she is she's burning it!" cried Uncle Wiggily suddenly. "For it's a burning smell that makes my pink nose twinkle!

Oh, look, Woodie!" the bunny exclaimed a moment later. "My bungalow is on fire! Oh, we must save Nurse Jane!"

Surely enough, as the bunny and groundhog turned a corner, they saw the bungalow; and clouds of black smoke were pouring from the windows! Uncle Wiggily dropped the bag string he was pulling on, hopped to his house and shouted:

"Oh, Nurse Jane! Nurse Jane! Where are you?"

"Up here!" cried the muskrat lady, thrusting her head from the second story window. "Oh, Wiggy the pies caught fire!"

"Never mind the pies—save yourself—jump out of the window!" shouted the rabbit.

"What's that?" asked the muskrat lady. "What was that you said, Uncle Wiggily? Did you tell me never to mind about the pies?"

"That's what I said," answered the bunny rabbit gentleman, and he was so excited that his pink nose twinkled backward, something which it hardly ever did. Perhaps the smoke caused it this time. "Don't mind about the pies, Janie!" he shouted at his muskrat lady housekeeper. "It is easy enough to get more pies, but if I lost you I would never have another Miss Fuzzy Wuzzy."

"That is very nice of you to say—ahem—a-ker-choo!" coughed and sneezed Nurse Jane, for she had swallowed some smoke. "I mean it is nice for you to speak of me in that way. But I don't like the way you talk about my pies. I go to a lot of work making pies, I put them in the oven to bake and when they catch fire—ahem—a-ker-choo!"

"Listen, Nurse Jane," shouted Uncle Wiggily. "I like to hear you talk, as well as anyone, but if you don't jump out of

that window pretty soon you'll be like the pies—all burned!
Jump! Jump, I say, and save yourself! Never mind the
pies! Never mind the bungalow! Never mind going back
for a clean handkerchief!" he shouted as he saw the muskrat
lady turning as if to go back into the burning place. "Jump,
Nurse Jane! Jump!"

She landed safely

"No! Don't jump yet! Wait a second!" yelled Woodie.
"Here, help me drag the bag of clover under the window for
Nurse Jane to jump on!" the groundhog boy called to Mr.
Longears. "If she lands on the soft clover she won't hurt
herself!"

"True enough! I forgot that!" cried Uncle Wiggily. Running back, he helped Woodie pull the bag of clover under the window. The smoke was almost choking Nurse Jane as she jumped. But she landed safely on the clover bag, bounced up once or twice like a rubber ball, bounced down again, and then she sobbed:

"Oh, my lovely pies! Oh, my dear bungalow! All burned!"

"Never mind the bungalow as long as you are safe!" said Uncle Wiggily. "But here come the water bugs! They'll soon have the fire out!"

Up came the water bugs of the fire department. Into the bungalow they swarmed, and soon the fire, which had started among the pies in the oven, was well soaked and squelched.

"Ha! Our bungalow isn't burned much after all!" observed Uncle Wiggily when the fire was out, and all the neighbors had gathered around. "There was more smoke than anything else. But it's a good thing Woodie had his bag of clover, or Nurse Jane might have been hurt when she jumped."

"And then she couldn't bake any more pies; could she?" asked Waddie Chuck, who, with Uncle Booster, the old groundhog gentleman, had run over to help put out the fire.

Everyone laughed at this, and Woodie and Waddie wondered why, because they were fond of pie, not to say cake.

"That's right," remarked Grandpa Whackum, the beaver gentleman, who had run over from the mill pond, when he heard that Uncle Wiggily's bungalow was on fire. "That certainly is right. No Nurse Jane—no pies."

"But, Uncle Wiggily," went on the old beaver gentleman,

whacking his tail down hard on the ground as he always did when he was excited, "why didn't you send for me when you found your place was all blazing?"

"Well, I'm glad nothing very serious happened," said Uncle Wiggily as the last of the smoke blew away.

"But something serious is going to happen right now!" suddenly cried a most unpleasant voice. "This is the best chance I'll ever get to nibble your ears, I think! Here I come!"

"Oh, Uncle Wiggily! Uncle Wiggily!" cried Woodie, from where he stood beside the clover bag. "There's a bad animal coming! Run in the bungalow and get something to drive him away! Quick! Here he comes!"

Uncle Wiggily just had time to run in, grab something and run out when, ALL OF A SUDDEN, the Pipsisewah ran hard to catch the bunny gentleman.

But Uncle Wiggily opened the bottle of olive oil he had taken from the bungalow, and poured it on the road. The bad Pipsisewah slipped and slid down the hill.

"There you go Pip!" laughed the rabbit. "Have an olive oil slide!"

"Good! Good!" cried Nurse Jane, when she saw what had taken place. "I always knew you were smart and clever, Wiggy! And I'm glad this part of your adventure happened near the bungalow so I could see it."

"I'm glad, also," said the bunny with a low and polite bow, after the bad animal had run away, without hurting him. "I wish you could have seen some of the other adventures I had, Nurse Jane."

"Well, some day, maybe, I'll come adventuring with you," promised the muskrat lady. "But now, as the smoke from the burned pies is all gone, and as there wasn't much of a fire after all, I'm going to bake an orange pudding for Woodie, Waddie and all our friends."

"Hurray!" cried the groundhog boys and all the other animals.

"Hurray!" cried Uncle Wiggily. "Everything happens for the best!"

"Hurray!" chuckled Uncle Booster.

And what a jolly time they had!

So if the piece of paper doesn't try to swim through the ink bottle and get so black that the stove pipe imagines it's a second cousin, I'll tell you next about Uncle Wiggily and Sammie's kite.

STORY XVII

UNCLE WIGGILY AND SAMMIE'S KITE

"Will you please make me a kite with a tail on, Uncle Wiggily?" begged Sammie the rabbit boy one day.

"Why do you want a kite with a tail on, when the kites without tails go up so much more easily?" asked Uncle Wiggily.

"Oh, I like to see the kite tail twisting up in the air like a snake," said Sammie.

So Uncle Wiggily made him a kite with a long tail to it, and after it was made Mr. Longears helped the little rabbit boy to fly the kite. It wasn't easy, as at first the tail was not heavy enough, and the kite dived from side to side like a hawk after a chicken.

Then Sammie made the tail too heavy and the kite would hardly go up at all. But at last the tail was made just about right and the kite went flying up into the air, slowly darting here and there and "jiggling the tail like a snake," as Sammie said.

"Well, I'll leave you for a while, Sammie," said Uncle Wiggily, "as I have to go to the store for Nurse Jane."

So Uncle Wiggily hopped to the five and six cent store to get ten cents worth of molasses sewing silk for his muskrat lady housekeeper, and Sammie kept on flying his kite.

On the way to the store Uncle Wiggily met Mr. Twistytail, the pig gentleman, who was also a barber.

162

"Where are you going, Mr. Twistytail?" asked Uncle Wiggily.

"I have just made a wig of very fine curled hair," said Mr. Twistytail, "and I am taking the wig to the bald eagle."

"I didn't know you made wigs for bald eagles," spoke Uncle Wiggily.

"Why, yes, of course I do," grunted the pig gentleman. "Don't you remember the song: 'Barber, barber, shave a pig. How many hairs will make a wig? Four and twenty—that's enough. Give the barber a pinch of snuff.'"

"Yes, I remember that," said Uncle Wiggily.

"Well," went on Mr. Twistytail, "the bald eagle gave me a pinch of snuff—aker-choo—excuse me, but every time I think of snuff I have to sneeze. The bald eagle gave me a pinch of snuff—aker-choo—excuse me. The bald eagle gave me a pinch of snuff—aker-choo—excuse me——"

"Say, look here," laughed Uncle Wiggily. "Never mind about the—well—never mind about—you know what—go on with your story."

"Well!" grunted Mr. Twistytail. "The bald eagle—no, I'll not say it—anyhow here's the wig I made for him," and he held it up. "I'm taking it to him now," he said. "You know the bald eagle doesn't like it that no hairs grow on the top of his head in the place where the hairs ought to grow, so he's going to wear a wig."

"It is very kind of you to make it for him," spoke the bunny.

"Well," grunted the pig, "the bald eagle gave me a pinch of snuff and—aker-choo—excuse me——"

But Uncle Wiggily, laughing, hopped on his way, leaving Mr. Twistytail to sneeze as much as he liked and take the wig to the bald eagle.

It was some little time after this—later in the day—that Uncle Wiggily met the pig gentleman again.

"Say, Uncle Wiggily, look here if you please! What kind of tricks do you call these?" and Mr. Twistytail puffed out his cheeks and seemed a very angry pig, indeed.

"Tricks? What do you mean?" asked the bunny gentleman. "I have been playing no tricks on you. Where's the bald eagle's wig?"

"That's just it—where is it?" grunted the gentleman pig. "If you haven't played a trick it's that rabbit nephew of yours, Sammie Littletail! Oh, dear me—snuff—ker-choo—excuse me—wigs! Oh, dear!"

"Why, whatever is the matter?" asked Uncle Wiggily.

"Well," went on Mr. Twistytail, "as I was walking through the wood taking the wig to the bald eagle, all of a sudden it was snatched from my paws, and right after that I saw Sammie running away as fast as he could run. He took my ker-choo—I mean my snuff—I mean the wig!"

"I hardly think Sammie would play a trick like that," said Uncle Wiggily, "but we'll go ask him." They found the little rabbit boy flying his kite with the tail on.

"Oh, no, Uncle Wiggily, I didn't take Mr. Twistytail's wig!" protested Sammie. "My kite dived down a little and I ran to get it back up again, but——".

"Pull down your kite for a moment, Sammie," said Uncle

Wiggily. And when this was done—lo and behold! There on the end of the kite tail was the bald eagle's wig.

"That's how it happened, Mr. Twistytail," said Uncle Wiggily. "Sammie's kite dived down, the tail tangled in the wig you carried and snatched it out of your paws. You saw Sammie running to get his kite up again."

"Oh, all right! Ho! Ha! That's a funny joke!" laughed the pig gentleman. "Anyhow I'm glad I have the bald eagle's wig back, and here is a penny to buy you a lollypop, Sammie."

"Thank you," laughed Sammie as he flew his kite without the wig. And if the parlor rug doesn't tickle the little toe on the foot of the stairs and make the rubber ball slide down the banister, I'll tell you next about Uncle Wiggily and the baby's bottle.

STORY XVIII

UNCLE WIGGILY AND BABY'S BOTTLE

"Oh, Mrs. Twistytail! How do you do?" exclaimed Nurse Jane Fuzzy Wuzzy one day, as she hurried down the steps of the hollow stump bungalow. Mrs. Twistytail, the lady pig, was coming along wheeling a baby carriage.

"I am quite well, Nurse Jane, and how are you?" asked Mrs. Twistytail, with a polite grunt as she wrinkled up her rubbery nose.

"Oh, I'm just wonderful!" squeaked the muskrat lady housekeeper. "And how is the dear baby?" For Mrs. Twistytail had a little baby pig in the carriage, you must know.

"Baby is very well—a little bit restless and fretful, for she is cutting teeth," said the lady pig, "'but not so very cross."

"Can't you come to the movies with me?" asked Nurse Jane. "They have a lovely picture there called, 'The Mystery of the Cheese Cake.' I'm just crazy to see it."

"I'd like to see it," grunted Mrs. Twistytail, "but I can't take Baby and I can't leave her alone, so——"

"I'll look after the baby for you, Mrs. Twistytail," offered Uncle Wiggily, who was sitting at an open window of the bungalow. "Go on to the picture with Nurse Jane. I've seen it, so I'll take care of Baby for you."

"I'm sure it is very kind of you, Uncle Wiggily," spoke Mrs. Twistytail. "I would like to go with Nurse Jane.

166

Baby will give you no trouble. She will sleep most of the time. But if she should happen to awaken just give her the bottle. It's in the carriage all filled with sour milk."

"Yes, that's so; little pigs like sour milk," murmured the bunny rabbit gentleman. "All right, ladies, toddle on and I'll look after the baby pig."

So Mrs. Twistytail and Nurse Jane went to the movies to see the Cheese Cake picture and Uncle Wiggily sat down near the carriage to twinkle his pink nose and watch Baby Twistytail.

At first nothing happened, but, after a while, when a fly had tickled Uncle Wiggily's pink nose two or three times, there was a movement in the carriage and Baby said:

"Wah!"

"Hum! I wonder what that means?" thought Uncle Wiggily; but not knowing much about pig talk he couldn't be sure what it was. Then, after a while, the Baby grunted:

"Go-goo! Gah! Zung!"

"Hum! That's different," said Uncle Wiggily, after listening carefully. "I guess she must want her bottle." So he hunted around in the blankets of the carriage until he found the bottle of sour milk with a rubber nipple on the end. The rabbit gentleman handed the bottle of milk to Baby Twistytail. She put the rubber nipple in her mouth and said:

"Gurr! Gurr!" Then she smiled at Uncle Wiggily.

"I guess that's what she wanted," thought Mr. Longears, and he turned away to take a little sleep in the shade, when, all of a sudden, a stream of sour milk struck him in the eye.

"Oh, my goodness!" exclaimed Uncle Wiggily, wiping the sour milk from his eye.

"Gurr! Gurr! Ha Ha!" laughed Baby Twistytail. At least it sounded as if she were laughing. And when the bunny gentleman looked at her, Baby had the nipple end of the bottle pointing right at him. Then she squeezed the rubber, as you squeeze a rubber ball full of water, and—"zing!" more sour milk squirted out and splashed Uncle Wiggily in his other eye.

"Oh, my goodness, Baby! You mustn't do that! Naughty! Naughty!" scolded Mr. Longears.

"Zu! Zu! Wah!" murmured the baby pig, and she squeezed the rubber end of her bottle again, and—"zing" more sour milk trickled down Uncle Wiggily's neck!

"Oh, stop it!" begged the bunny uncle. "Take your lunch, Baby Pig, and don't be naughty!"

"Ha! Speaking of lunches, it's time for mine!" suddenly cried a harsh voice, "and my lunch is going to be nibbled ears!" And with that out from the bushes jumped the Fuzzy Fox.

"Gurr! Zing! Ga! Woo!" yelled Baby Twistytail, and then she aimed her bottle straight at the Fox and pressed on the rubber nipple!

"Zip!" a stream of sour milk struck the Fox in both eyes at once.

"Oh, Wowzie Wow!" howled the bad chap. "I never expected this!" And he ran around in a circle and turned a somersault and then he flopped away off in the woods, wiping the sour milk from his eyes as he ran, so he didn't nibble any ears that day.

"Baby, you are a good little pig," said Uncle Wiggily.

"Gurr! Goo!" murmured little Miss Twistytail, and then she went to sleep. And if the pancake doesn't turn upside down after the maple syrup has gone to sleep on it, I'll tell you next about Uncle Wiggily and the bonfire.

STORY XIX

UNCLE WIGGILY'S BONFIRE

"Uncle Wiggily, what is a b-u-n fire?" asked Baby Bunty, the little rabbit girl, one day, when she had come visiting to the hollow stump bungalow.

"A bun fire?" repeated Uncle Wiggily. "Well, I should say a bun fire was a fire where you burned buns."

"How silly!" exclaimed Nurse Jane Fuzzy Wuzzy, the muskrat lady housekeeper. "Whoever heard of burning buns! What's all this, anyhow, about a bun fire?"

"I was just reading about it in my story book," said Baby Bunty. "It says they built a bun fire and had lots of fun."

"Oh, she means a BON fire!" laughed Nurse Jane. "Bon is a French word, Baby Bunty, meaning good, and when they first built those fires it was because something good had happened. Something jolly, you know."

"Yes'm," spoke Baby Bunty. "I guess I spelled it wrong. But I'd like a jolly bonfire, Uncle Wiggily. Couldn't you make me one?"

"Why, I s'pose I could," answered the rabbit gentleman, slowly. "We could make a bonfire, you and I, Baby Bunty, and roast apples in it."

"I thought it would be something like this," sighed Nurse Jane. "You are more of a child than ever, Wiggy. Building bonfires at your age! And I was going to ask you to go to the store for me."

170

"I'll go!" quickly offered Uncle Wiggily. "What is it you want?"

"Molasses," answered the muskrat lady. "I want to make a molasses pie."

"Then molasses you shall have," sang Uncle Wiggily, twinkling his pink nose. "And on the way home Baby Bunty and I will build a bonfire and roast apples."

So the bunny gentleman and the little rabbit girl started off, and in a little while they were at the molasses store.

"I thought you were going to build a bonfire," complained Baby Bunty.

"I am," said Uncle Wiggily. "But business before pleasure, you know. It is business to get Nurse Jane the molasses. Now that we have it, we shall take pleasure in building the bonfire."

So, carrying the jug of molasses, Uncle Wiggily and Baby Bunty hopped along until they came to a place where there was some wood and dried leaves. And it was right on the edge of an apple orchard.

"This is a dandy place to make a bonfire," said the rabbit gentleman. "You sit down on the grass, Bunty, and keep out of the way of burning sparks. I'll make the fire."

Soon the rabbit gentleman had a cheerful blaze snapping and cracking under an apple tree. And when the fire was blazing hot, he placed in the glowing embers some apples that he had picked up off the ground, apples the farmer man didn't want.

"How long before they will be ready to eat?" asked Baby Bunty.

"Oh, in about ten minutes, I guess," Uncle Wiggily answered.

"Ho! Ho!" suddenly cried a harsh voice behind the apple tree. "I know something that will be ready to eat in less than ten minutes! Ho! Ho!"

"What do you mean?" asked Uncle Wiggily, before he had time to think.

"I mean your ears," howled the voice of the Woozie Wolf, as he sprang out from behind the tree. "I am going to nibble your ears and I am not going to wait ten minutes, either!"

"Oh, my goodness!" shouted Baby Bunty. And then, being a lively, smart little rabbit girl, instead of fainting as a wax doll would have done, Baby Bunty began to think of a way to save Uncle Wiggily's ears.

The Woozie Wolf was just leaping to catch the bunny rabbit gentleman, when Baby Bunty threw a lot of wet leaves on the bonfire. The wet leaves made a cloud of thick smoke, which blew in the eyes of the bad Wolf.

"Where are you? Ker-choo! Ker-snoo!" sneezed the Wolf. "I can't see you, Uncle Wiggily! Where are you?"

"Don't say a word," whispered Baby Bunty, as she pulled Uncle Wiggily behind a cloud of thick, white smoke. "Keep still and he can't find us!"

The Wolf went lumbering around, coughing, choking and sneezing, besides hic-coughing, as the smoke got in his eyes, but he couldn't find the bunny rabbit. Then, all of a sudden, Uncle Wiggily looked through the cloud of smoke and he saw the end of the Wolf's tail turned toward him.

"Stick some molasses on his tail!" whispered Bunty.

"I will!" said Uncle Wiggily, and he did. And when the Wolf felt the sticky molasses dribbling on his tail he howled and yowled and ran through the smoke, banging his nose on a tree. Then he howled louder than ever and ran back in the woods where he belonged.

"Now he's gone, we can eat our baked apples," said Baby Bunty, which she and Uncle Wiggily did after the smoke blew away.

They had a jolly good time, and the molasses pie Nurse Jane made was most delicious. And if the chocolate cake doesn't try to go swimming with the gold fish and catch cold, I'll tell you next about Uncle Wiggily and the big wind.

STORY XX

UNCLE WIGGILY AND THE BIG WIND

The Woozie Wolf sat on his hind legs in the den of the Fuzzy Fox and blinked his eyes.

"I'm hungry!" snarled the Woozie Wolf.

"So am I!" growled the Fuzzy Fox.

"It may seem impolite of me not to ask you to stay to lunch," he went on, "but the truth of the matter is that my cupboard is bare—like Mother Hubbard's."

"So is mine—not a thing to eat in the house!" snarled the Wolf. "We simply must get something. I know what I'm going to do!"

"What?" asked the Fox, eagerly.

"I'm going to nibble Uncle Wiggily's ears," said the Wolf.

"Ha! Ha! Ha! Oh, that is funny!" laughed the Fox. "We have tried, forty-'leven times, to get that rabbit's ears, and never once have we done it."

"I shall get them this time!" snapped the Wolf. "Just you wait and I'll show you."

Out of the den of the Fox slipped the Woozie Wolf. He seemed so much in earnest that the Fox trotted after him.

"I say, old dear," whispered the Fox, "if there's really anything in this, you know, you ought to let me share. We're partners and buddies, you remember."

"Come along if you like," invited the Wolf, indifferent like.

174

So the Fox and the Wolf tramped through the woods together, getting more and more hungry all the while. Soon they were near the hollow stump bungalow of the rabbit gentleman.

"What new plan are you going to try to nibble Uncle Wiggily's ears?" asked the Fox. "We have tried so many, only to see them all fail, that I haven't much hope."

"We'll get him this time," snarled the Wolf. "When you see a bush with big, long, stickery, prickery thorns on let me know."

"Good gracious!" barked the Fox. "You can't pin Uncle Wiggily fast with a sharp thorn. He'll jump over your head."

"Never mind about that," went on the Wolf. "Just tell me when you see a thorn bush."

Pretty soon they slunk past a thorn bush and the Fox said: "There it is!"

"Good!" snapped the Wolf. "Now pick the longest thorn you can find and I'll do the same."

So the Wolf had a thorn and the Fox had a thorn—long, sharp, stickery, prickery thorns from the thorn bush.

Pretty soon the Fox looked down the hill and he saw Uncle Wiggily riding along in his automobile, with big bologna sausage tires on the wheels, filled with lots of air.

"There goes our rabbit now," said the Fox. "He's riding away from us. How are we going to get his ears?"

"Come along!" howled the Wolf. "He won't ride forever. He has to stop some time. Come on!"

So the Fox and the Wolf, with their long, sharp, stickery,

prickery thorns, raced on after the bunny gentleman in his automobile.

In a little while Uncle Wiggily stopped at the house of Mrs. Twistytail, the lady pig. He was going to give her a piece of coffee pie Nurse Jane had sent over.

"There, you see!" whispered the Wolf to the Fox. "He is stopping! Now we can play the trick on him and get his ears."

"What is the trick?" asked the Fox.

"Just this," answered the Wolf. "While Uncle Wiggily is in Mrs. Twistytail's house we'll slip up behind his auto and jab our sharp thorns in his tires. This will make them flat, and when he comes out to ride away he can't go. Then we can easily nibble his ears."

"It sounds like a good trick," said the Fox. Though I think it was rather a bad one. However, when Uncle Wiggily was in the pig lady's house, the Fox and Wolf slipped up. Standing behind the big tires of the hind wheels, the bad chaps jabbed in their thorns.

"Boom! Hiss! Wuff!"

Out rushed the air, and it was so strong that it blew the Fox and Wolf head over heels, across the tree tops away back in the woods.

"My goodness! What a big wind must be blowing!" cried the bunny uncle, as he was looking from Mrs. Twistytail's window. "Such a big, strong wind, it blew the Fox and Wolf away. I think they were coming after me!"

"I don't hear any wind blowing," said the lady pig. And,

surely enough, when they went out, the wind wasn't blowing at all. But the bunny had two flat tires.

"Ah, I know what happened," he laughed, when he saw the thorns still sticking in the rubber. "It was a trick! But the Fox and Wolf didn't know I had a lot of wind in my tires this time, instead of bologna sausage. My, how far away they were blown! Ha! Ha!"

So the bad chaps didn't nibble any ears after all. And when the bunny had mended the holes in his tires he rode on again. And if the five-cent piece doesn't jump through the hole in the penny and turn into a dime, I'll tell you next about Uncle Wiggily and the white shoes.

STORY XXI

UNCLE WIGGILY AND THE WHITE SHOES

Once upon a time Nurse Jane Fuzzy Wuzzy, the muskrat lady housekeeper for Uncle Wiggily sat in the hollow stump bungalow, sadly looking at a pair of soiled, white shoes. The shoes were quite dirty, spicked, spotted and spattered.

"Oh, dear!" sighed Nurse Jane, "I don't know what to do about these white shoes."

"What about them?" asked the bunny rabbit gentleman. "They only need cleaning with some of that white stuff you put on during the summer."

"That's just the trouble," went on Nurse Jane. "I do so dislike to clean white shoes, and yet I don't want to buy a new pair so late in the season. But I need a pair of clean white shoes to wear to Mrs. Wibblewobble's picnic. Dear me! I don't know what to do!"

"Perhaps you could borrow a pair of white shoes from some of your lady friends," said Uncle Wiggily. "Mrs. Twistytail, the pig lady, or Mrs. Ringtail, the raccoon lady may have a pair of white shoes that are cleaner than yours."

"It's a good idea—I'll try it," said Nurse Jane. "I'll go over and ask Mrs. Twistytail."

She was gone only a short time before she came back looking more sad than ever.

"Didn't Mrs. Twistytail have any white shoes?" asked the bunny.

"Yes, but they were so large my feet slipped all over in them like roller skates," said Nurse Jane. "I'll go over and see what Mrs. Ringtail has. She is about my size."

And when Nurse Jane was gone Uncle Wiggily looked at his muskrat lady housekeeper's soiled white shoes.

"I think I'll surprise Miss Fuzzy Wuzzy," said the rabbit gentleman. "She would much rather wear her own shoes if they were only clean and white, so I'll clean and whiten them for her. I don't mind getting my paws all covered with chalk dust."

No sooner said than done. Uncle Wiggily took Nurse Jane's shoes out on the back steps with a bottle of the white cleaning stuff and he set to work. He had one shoe partly whitened and was thinking what jolly fun it was—almost like an adventure—when, all of a sudden, Jackie Bow Wow, the puppy dog boy, came around the corner of the hollow stump bungalow.

"Oh, Uncle Wiggily!" barked Jackie, and then, all of a sudden he stopped. A queer look came over his face. Jackie opened his mouth wide and he gasped. "Oh-er-um! Ah! Wha-wha-what in the world——?"

Then he tucked his tail between his legs and ran away as fast as he could run.

"My goodness!" laughed Uncle Wiggily. "I wonder what's the matter with Jackie? He must have forgotten to go to the store for his mother and he thought of it just as he got here to ask me to go adventuring with him, I suppose. Ah, puppies will be puppies! And now for the other shoe. The first one is clean and white!"

Uncle Wiggily had almost finished the other shoe when around the corner of the hollow stump bungalow crept Tommie Kat, the pussy boy.

"Oh, Uncle Wiggily!" mewed Tommie. Then his tail fluffed up big and he cried:

"Wow! Wow! Zing! Oh, my goodness!" And away he ran.

"This is strange!" thought the bunny. "Tommie also must have forgotten something. Well, I must finish this shoe," so he kept on whitening it.

Tommie and Jackie ran along the street until they reached the office of Dr. Possum, who cured the sick animals.

"Oh, Dr. Possum!" barked Jackie. "You should go to see Uncle Wiggily at once! He is very sick!"

"Terrible!" mewed Tommie. "He's got the epizootic, or something!"

"I'll go right away! I'll take the ambulance with me," said Dr. Possum, "and ride him off to the hospital. You may ride on the ambulance with me, boys!"

So Dr. Possum and the animal boys rode on the cling-clanging ambulance to the hollow stump bungalow. On the way many of the animal friends of Uncle Wiggily saw the ambulance going to his house, so they ran along, following it. With a cling and a clang of the bell the ambulance stopped in front of the rabbit's bungalow.

"Come to the hospital with me at once, Uncle Wiggily!" cried Dr. Possum, when the bunny gentleman had opened the door. "Oh, how dreadfully ill you look!"

"Why, I'm not sick at all! What's the matter with you?"

cried Uncle Wiggily. "Why have you the ambulance? Why is the crowd here? Why——".

"You're as white as a sheet!" said Dr. Possum. "You're pale! Even your pink nose is pale, and so are your paws and so are your whiskers! You're pale all over!"

Uncle Wiggily looked in the glass. Then he laughed, "Ha! Ha! Ho! Ho!" and he said: "Pale! I'm not pale! That's the white stuff from cleaning Nurse Jane's shoes! I guess I did get some on my pink nose!"

"White stuff! Nurse Jane's shoes! Is that all it is?" asked Dr. Possum. And when he looked closer and rubbed some of the white stuff off the bunny he, too, had to laugh.

"Well, he certainly did look sick," said Jackie and Tommie.

"Never mind, boys, you meant it very kindly," chuckled Uncle Wiggily, as he finished cleaning the shoes. And it was well he did, for Nurse Jane couldn't wear Mrs. Ring-tail's. So everything happened for the best. And if the hair brush doesn't try to go roller skating on the looking glass and spill the talcum powder, I'll tell you next about Uncle Wiggily and Bunty's ball.

STORY XXII

UNCLE WIGGILY AND BUNTY'S BALL

"Uncle Wiggily! Oh, Uncle Wiggily!" called a voice behind the bunny rabbit gentleman, as he was hopping along the woodland path one morning.

"My gracious goodness! I hope this isn't the Fuzzy Fox or the Wuzzy Wolf after me so early!" thought Uncle Wiggily. But when he turned around he saw Baby Bunty, the little rabbit girl, hopping along.

"What's the matter, Baby Bunty?" asked Uncle Wiggily. "Are you afraid?" For she was hopping very fast.

"Yes, I—I am a little afraid," said Bunty.

"What are you afraid of?" asked Mr. Longears, for he could see nothing to frighten any one.

"I am afraid you won't give me five cents if I ask you for it; will you?" And Baby Bunty shyly looked down to see if she had lost any buttons off her lace shoes, but she hadn't, I'm glad to say.

"You're afraid I won't give you five cents," wonderingly repeated Uncle Wiggily. "But why should you want five cents, Bunty?"

"To buy a rubber ball to squirt water," answered the little rabbit girl. "If you give me five cents I can buy a rubber ball to squirt water right next to the hollow stump school and I'll have lots of fun."

"You wouldn't squirt water in school, would you, Baby Bunty?" asked the bunny gentleman.

"Oh, no! Of course not! Why, the very idea!" gasped Baby Bunty. "If I did, the Lady Mouse Teacher would keep me in after school. Oh, no, I wouldn't do such a thing as that—never! never! never!" and Baby Bunty shook her head so hard that she nearly shook off her pink blue hair ribbon.

"All right then, here's the five cents to buy the rubber ball to squirt water," said Mr. Longears.

"Now I'm not afraid any more!" laughed Baby Bunty, as she skipped along to school. Uncle Wiggily stood watching her for a while, his pink nose twinkling sort of sideways, and then he hopped along to look for an adventure.

But adventures were rather scarce that morning, like hens' teeth you know, and after a while Uncle Wiggily said to himself:

"I think I'll hop along and visit the hollow stump school. The Lady Mouse Teacher is always glad to see me, and it will be just as well to take a look in and see that Baby Bunty isn't squirting her water rubber ball. If she did Teacher would blame me for giving Bunty the money to buy it."

Uncle Wiggily hopped along and along and along until he was at the hollow stump school, and then he hopped inside where the animal children were studying and reciting their lessons.

"Oh good morning, Uncle Wiggily!" greeted the Lady Mouse Teacher. "We are very glad to see you; aren't we children?"

"Yes, teacher, we are very glad to see Uncle Wiggily!"

said all the animal boys and girls together, like clocks ticking and tocking.

"Sit down in this chair on my platform," said the Lady Mouse Teacher, "and I will have the children sing a song for you, Uncle Wiggily."

So the rabbit gentleman sat down in the chair and the children sang.

First they sang the song about "Once a Cheese Was Baited with a Piece of Trap," and after that they sang, "Squinkle, Squinkle, Little Tar, I Love You No Matter How Black You Are." Both were very pretty songs.

But, all the while, Uncle Wiggily was watching Baby Bunty, for he feared lest the little rabbit girl might squirt water from the rubber ball and so be kept in after school. But Baby seemed to be very good indeed. And once she pointed with her paw to the top of her desk, and Uncle Wiggily, looking, saw the rubber ball asleep there.

"I guess Bunty is going to be good and not squirt her ball," thought Mr. Longears. Then the Lady Mouse Teacher squeaked:

"Baby Bunty, you may now stand up near your desk and recite the little poem for your Uncle Wiggily." So Bunty recited about "Little Boy Red, Who Stood on His Head." It was a funny little verse.

Bunty made her final bow and sat down in her seat. And as she did so, a stream of water squirted out and struck Floppy Twistytail, the piggie boy, right in the ear! Right in Floppy's ear squirted the water.

"Oh, wee! Wee! Squee! Squee!" howled Floppy. "Oh,

Baby Bunty squirted water on me from her rubber ball!" he howled.

"Baby Bunty! Did you do that?" asked the Lady Mouse Teacher sadly.

"The worst has happened!" thought Uncle Wiggily, his pink nose trembling.

"Teacher, I didn't do it on purpose," said Baby Bunty. "My rubber ball, full of water, was on top of my desk. It rolled down into my seat and when I sat down, I sat on the rubber ball, accidental like, and squashed it, and that made it squirt on Floppy."

"Oh, that's all right, if it was an accident," kindly said the Lady Mouse. "But don't do it again, Bunty."

"No'm," said Bunty. And then all the other animal children laughed, and so did the little boy pig, for the water didn't hurt him, and the Lady Mouse and Uncle Wiggily laughed also.

"But I surely thought Bunty did it on purpose," said Mr. Longears to Nurse Jane that night.

"Maybe she did," laughed Miss Fuzzy Wuzzy, "but I hardly think so; do you?" And if the little poodle dog doesn't waggle his tail in the ink bottle and try to write his name on the wallpaper, I'll tell you next about Uncle Wiggily and the hickory nuts.

STORY XXIII

UNCLE WIGGILY'S HICKORY NUTS

Far, far off in the dark and dismal woods sat the Fuzzy Fox, the Woozie Wolf and the Skillery Scallery Alligator with humps on his tail. They were talking about how to catch Uncle Wiggily so they might nibble his ears.

"I'll tell you what is," gargled the Alligator, "you may be very smart and clever, Mr. Fox and Mr. Wolf, but you have been trying to catch Uncle Wiggily in the wrong way."

"The wrong way? What do you mean?" growled the Wolf.

"Yes, tell us what you mean," snarled the Fox.

"Well," said the 'Gator, "you always use your front paws or your teeth in trying to catch that rabbit, and he always gets away from you."

"How else should we try to catch him, except with our claws or teeth?" asked the Fox.

"You should use your tails once in a while," said the Alligator. "I always use my tail when I want to catch anything. I knock down with my tail any rabbit or squirrel I want to catch. And when I knock them down they are so surprised that I can easily catch them. You should do that with Uncle Wiggily."

"Pooh! Pooh!" laughed the Fox.

"Nonsense!" snapped the Wolf. "That may be all right

186

for you, Mr. 'Gator, for your tail is knobby and humpy with lumps on it. But our tails are soft, like dusting brushes."

"That's right," yapped the Fox. "I should like to see you, Mr. 'Gator, catch Uncle Wiggily just by switching your tail around. I'd like to see you do it."

"Very well, you shall," said the Alligator. "I'll catch that rabbit, and I'll be kind and generous to you and let you each take some teeny weeny nibbles from his ears."

"Ha! Ha!" laughed the Fox.

"Ho! Ho!" laughed the Wolf.

"I'll show you," bellowed the Skillery Scallery Alligator with the humps on his tail.

Not long after this Uncle Wiggily started away from his hollow stump bungalow.

"Where are you going?" asked Nurse Jane Fuzzy Wuzzy, his muskrat lady housekeeper.

"I am going to gather hickory nuts from the hickory nut tree in the dark and dismal forest," answered Uncle Wiggily.

"What for?" asked Nurse Jane. "Your teeth are not strong enough to crack the hard hickory nuts. They are only good for squirrels like Johnnie and Billie Bushytail."

"And it is for Johnnie and Billie Bushytail that I am going to gather the hickory nuts from the hickory nut tree in the dark and dismal forest," said Uncle Wiggily. "The little squirrel boys have the mumps, and I am going to get them some hickory nuts."

"I wouldn't think hickory nuts could cure the mumps," said Nurse Jane, "but perhaps you know best."

So Uncle Wiggily started off to gather hickory nuts from

the hickory nut tree in the dark and dismal forest. And, as he left his hollow stump bungalow the bunny rabbit gentleman was seen by the Skillery Scallery Alligator with humps on his tail.

"Oh, ho!" snickered the 'Gator, "this is my chance to catch Uncle Wiggily and show the Fox and Wolf what I can do with my tail. I am very smart. This time there shall be some ear nibbles."

The Alligator followed Uncle Wiggily to the dark and dismal forest. Pretty soon the bunny gentleman reached the hickory nut tree. But alas, the nuts were high up on the branches, and, as yet, there had been no frost to make them fall to the ground.

"I wonder how I can get some hickory nuts for Johnnie and Billie Bushytail?" asked the rabbit out loud.

"You must shake the tree," cawed a black crow flying in the air. "Shake the tree hard, Uncle Wiggily, and the nuts will fall."

So Uncle Wiggily took hold of the tree in his paws and tried to shake it, and just then the Skillery Scallery Alligator with humps on his tail crawled out of the bushes.

"Now is my chance!" hissed the 'Gator. "I'll knock Uncle Wiggily down with my tail and surprise him so that I can carry him off to the Fox and Wolf and we'll nibble his ears."

So the 'Gator bent back his tail to hit Uncle Wiggily a hard blow, but the Black Crow in the air over head saw him and called:

"Duck your head, Uncle Wiggily! Lean down and duck your head!"

The bunny rabbit gentleman, thinking the hickory nuts were going to fall on him, crouched down. Just then the 'Gator lashed out with his tail, but instead of hitting the rabbit, the 'Gator's tail hit the hickory nut tree a terrible whack.

"Clatter! Clatter! Rattle te bang!" down fell a thousand hickory nuts, for Uncle Wiggily hadn't shaken the tree enough to cause one to fall. Oh, what a blow the 'Gator's tail hit the tree!

"Wowchie! Ouchie! Wow!" howled the 'Gator. "My tail is broken entirely!" And, sick and sore, he limped off through the woods, not daring to try any more to catch the bunny.

"Ha! Ha!" laughed Uncle Wiggily as he stood up and saw the hickory nuts on the ground. "Thank you, Mr. Skillery Scallery Alligator! You knocked down a lot of nuts for me!"

And oh! how angry the Fox and Wolf were when the lame-tailed 'Gator limped back from the dark and dismal forest. But the bunny took the hickory nuts to the squirrel boys, who were soon cured of the mumps.

And if the piano doesn't step on the foot of the stairs when it's playing tag with the phonograph, I'll tell you next about Uncle Wiggily and the electric bell.

STORY XXIV

UNCLE WIGGILY'S ELECTRIC BELL

"Some one is at the door, Nurse Jane!" called Uncle Wiggily, soon after he reached his hollow stump bungalow, coming home from an adventure trip one day. "There goes the electric bell."

But the muskrat lady housekeeper sat still in her chair, knitting a buttonhole on one of Uncle Wiggily's socks.

"Aren't you going to the door?" asked the rabbit gentleman, as the electric bell rang still more loudly. "Aren't you going, Nurse Jane?"

"There is no use," answered Miss Fuzzy Wuzzy, as she sewed together two of Uncle Wiggily's old neckties to make a pair of shoe laces for the rag doll.

"Why not?" asked Mr. Longears. "Why don't you go to the door when the bell rings? That is, unless you're afraid and want me to go?" he asked, more boldly. "If you do—"

"Oh, not at all!" laughed Nurse Jane. "The fact of the matter is, Uncle Wiggily, that there isn't any one at the door."

"But I hear the bell ringing!" said the bunny gentleman. "Listen to it—tinkle, tinkle, tink!"

"Yes, I heard it," said Nurse Jane with a smile. "But it has been ringing like that all day, and whenever I go to the door no one is there. So I'm tired of going."

"If the bell rings, and there is no one there, it must be

190

some of the animal boys playing tricks," declared Uncle
Wiggily. "I'll catch the little rascals!" and he started for
the door, while the electric bell still rang.

"Don't trouble yourself," laughed the muskrat lady housekeeper. "I, also, thought it was some of the boys, but when
I slipped quietly to the door and looked out, no one was
there, but the bell still rang. It must be an invisible fairy."

"Nonsense!" laughed Uncle Wiggily. "It's just something the matter with the bell—that's all. I'll fix it."

So the bunny rabbit gentleman looked at the push button
on the front door. To make the electric bell ring this button
must be pushed. And when Uncle Wiggily put on his
glasses and looked at the front door button, he saw what the
trouble was.

"Someone," he said, "and it must have been one of the animal boys, has stuck a pin in the push button. This is just
the same as if they stood there all the while and kept pushing on the button. No wonder the bell rang all the while,
with the pin in the push button! I'll take it out."

Now, while Uncle Wiggily went back in his hollow stump
bungalow to get his hammer, saw, screw driver and pliers
with which to take the pin out of the push button, along came
the Bob Cat and the Fox. They were going to slip quietly
past Uncle Wiggily's bungalow, when the Bob Cat said:

"I have an idea, Mr. Fox."

"What is it?" asked the Fox.

"I have an idea," whispered the Bob Cat, "that if I were
to step up and ring Uncle Wiggily's bell, he might come to
the door before he knew who it was and I could grab him!"

"Nonsense!" snickered the Fox. "You can't catch a smart old rabbit like Uncle Wiggily in that fashion. Ring his bell! The idea! Stuff and nonsense!"

"All the same, I am going to try," said the Bob Cat. "I'll go up and ring his electric bell and when he comes to the door I'll grab him and nibble his ears!"

"Won't you give me any nibbles?" asked the Fox.

"I will if you help me ring the bell," said the Bob Cat.

"All right," agreed the Fox. "I'll push it once and you may push it once. Then we'll both grab Uncle Wiggily together!"

So the two bad animals went up the front steps of the bunny rabbit's hollow stump bungalow. Oh, so softly they went up and they were so excited that they never heard the electric bell inside ringing all the while. For, as yet, Uncle Wiggily had not taken the sharp pin from the push button.

On the steps stood the Fox and on the steps stood the Bob Cat.

"I'll push the button first!" said the Bob Cat and push it he did, as hard as he could. "Oh, wowchie! Ouchie! Oh, what a pain!" he howled as the pin stuck in his paw.

"Ha! Ha! You don't know how to push a bell button!" laughed the Fox. "I'll show you!" So the Fox pushed the electric button a great deal harder than the Bob Cat and the sharp-pointed pin went deeper into his paw. "Ouch! Wow! Zowie cars and jitney lollypops!" howled the Fox. Then he fell over backward in a somersault down the steps, knocking the Bob Cat head over heels, and away they ran.

"Ha! Ha!" laughed Uncle Wiggily as he came out to pull

the pin from the push button. "The boys' trick saved me from the bad chaps! Ha! Ha!" Then he pulled the pin from the button and the bell stopped ringing and all was well.

And if the rubber ball doesn't bounce up to look in the face of the clock and shake the hands, I'll tell you next about Uncle Wiggily and the red paint.

STORY XXV

UNCLE WIGGILY AND THE RED PAINT

"My goodness!" exclaimed Nurse Jane Fuzzy Wuzzy one day as she started out of the hollow stump bungalow. "They certainly are worn off and look very shabby!"

"Are you speaking of your gloves?" asked Uncle Wiggily, as he gave his pink nose a little twinkle on one side. "If you are, why, buy yourself a new pair and charge them to me. I don't want you to wear shabby gloves."

"Oh, I wasn't speaking of gloves," laughed Nurse Jane. "It was the front steps I meant. All the paint is worn off them and they look very shabby. I think, Uncle Wiggily, it would be well to have Grandpa Whacker, the beaver gentleman carpenter, paint them."

"I'll take a look," said Mr. Longears.

And when he had hopped to the front steps, using his red, white and blue striped rheumatism crutch to lean on, and when he had looked to where his muskrat lady housekeeper pointed, Uncle Wiggily said:

"Yes, indeed, the steps need painting, but I'll do it myself."

"Can you paint steps?" asked Nurse Jane.

"Of course I can," answered the bunny gentleman. "I'll hop to the store and get the paint. When you come back the steps will be as good as new. But you will have to go in the back way on account of wet paint."

194

"I shall not mind that," said Nurse Jane.

So off she went to the moving pictures with Mrs. Twisty-tail, the lady pig, while Uncle Wiggily hopped to the three and ten cent store to get some paint for the steps.

"What color paint do you want?" asked the little mousie girl clerk behind the counter.

"I'll take red paint because it is so cheerful," answered the rabbit gentleman, and soon he was hopping back to his hollow stump bungalow carrying the red paint and a brush with which to spread it on the front steps.

Uncle Wiggily began painting with the red paint, but he had not worked very long before he heard behind him a little voice asking:

"Oh, Uncle Wiggily, please let me paint a teeny bit!"

The rabbit gentleman turned around and there stood Baby Bunty, the tiny rabbit girl.

"Oh, no, Bunty! You couldn't paint!" laughed Uncle Wiggily. "You'd get the red stuff all over your dress! Run along and play!"

So Baby Bunty ran along to play and Uncle Wiggily kept on using the red paint, when, all of a sudden, another voice behind him asked:

"Please, couldn't I paint a little?"

The rabbit gentleman turned and there stood Jollie Long-tail, the mousie boy.

"Oh, my goodness, no! You couldn't paint, Jollie," said the bunny. "You'd get red paint all over your tail. Skip along and play ball."

So Jollie skipped along and played ball, and Uncle Wiggily kept on painting. Pretty soon another voice behind him asked:

"Uncle Wiggily, please couldn't I help you paint?"

The bunny rabbit turned and there stood Billie Wagtail, the goat.

"Oh, my goodness, no, Billie!" laughed Uncle Wiggily. "I couldn't let you take my red paint brush! You'd get red paint all over your horns! Scoot along and play tag!"

So Billie scooted along and he played tag and Uncle Wiggily kept on spreading red paint all over the front steps, making them look like a fire engine, bright and cheerful.

Then, after a while, not so very long, along came the Black Bushy Bear with his shining black nose.

"Ah, ha!" growled the Black Bushy Bear to himself. "This is my chance to nibble Uncle Wiggily's ears! I'll slip up behind him and ask him to let me paint. He'll think I'm one of the animal children and he'll hand me the brush. Then I'll slap it in his eyes, and fill them with red paint. And when he can't see I'll nibble his ears! Ho! Ho!"

A cruel trick it was, but let us see what happens. Up shuffled the Bear very quietly. Then making believe he was a cute little boy he said in a soft voice:

"Please, Uncle Wiggily, let me paint a weeny bit."

Uncle Wiggily, thinking it was Baby Bunty back again, or maybe Billie Wagtail, didn't turn his head. But the bunny gentleman said:

"Now you run along and play the piano! I can't let you paint. See, you might get all over red paint like this!"

And, without turning his head to look, Uncle Wiggily held out the brush behind him to show how red it was. And the Bear was so close to the bunny, ready to nibble his ears, that Uncle Wiggily slapped the brush, all covered with red paint, on the black, glistening nose of the Black Bushy Bear. All over red paint was the Bear's nose splashed!

"Oh, Guff, Wuff! Scuff! Ga-zinka!" howled the Bear when he looked down at his nose, cross-eyed, and saw that it was red. "Oh, my nose is on fire, it's so red!" he howled! And, being very proud of his black nose and not wanting it red, away ran the Bear to rub the red paint off his nose against a tree.

"Ha! Ha!" laughed Uncle Wiggily, as he turned and saw the Bear running away. "It's a good thing I painted his nose red as well as the steps! Ho! Ho!" Then he finished his work, and when Nurse Jane came back from the movies the steps looked like new—bright and red, like a fire engine going to a picnic. And how the muskrat lady laughed when the rabbit told her about the Bear's red nose.

And if the oil can doesn't take the roller skates away from the rocking horse and try to fly with them, I'll tell you next about Uncle Wiggily and runaway Bunty.

STORY XXVI

UNCLE WIGGILY AND RUNAWAY BUNTY

"Goodness me sakes alive!" sighed Nurse Jane Fuzzy Wuzzy one day, as Uncle Wiggily sat reading the Cabbage Leaf Gazette newspaper in the hollow stump bungalow. "I don't know what I'm going to do with her."

"What's the trouble now?" asked the rabbit gentleman, twinkling his pink nose because a little fly wanted to sit on it and get warm.

"It's Baby Bunty," answered the muskrat lady housekeeper. "She has run away again!"

"Run away again?" exclaimed Uncle Wiggily. "Do you mean to say she has run away before?"

"Oh, yes, many times," replied Miss Fuzzy Wuzzy. "I didn't tell you about it, for I didn't want you to worry, but Baby Bunty is getting to be a regular runaway and I can't seem to stop her."

"Hum!" said Uncle Wiggily. And then, once again, he said: "Hum!"

That meant he was thinking very hard.

"I shall have to do something to teach Baby Bunty not to run away so much," he said after a while.

"I wish you would," sighed Nurse Jane. Then Miss Fuzzy Wuzzy started out to hunt the lost, runaway Baby Bunty. And where do you think she was found?

Away off under the mulberry bush making mud pies with Kittie Kat, the pussy girl.

"Baby Bunty, why do you run away so much?" asked Nurse Jane sadly as she led the little rabbit girl back to the hollow stump bungalow.

"I don't know—just for fun, I guess," laughed Baby Bunty.

"Well, it isn't any laughing matter for me," said Nurse Jane. "You must not run away again, Bunty."

"No'm, I won't," said Baby Bunty. But as she always said this and nearly always ran away again next day, you couldn't put much trust in her.

Baby Bunty was a queer little rabbit girl. She was an orphan, like "Orphant Annie," and she used to live, in turn, at the homes of the other animals where she "washed an' wiped the dishes an' put th' cups away."

Baby Bunty was very cute, sweet and lovable, but she had this one fault—she would run away. No matter at whose home she was staying—whether at Uncle Wiggily's bungalow or at the cave of Mr. Whitewash, the jolly polar bear, Baby Bunty would run away.

"I must do something to cure her," thought Uncle Wiggily when Nurse Jane brought the little tyke home after her last trip. "I must teach Bunty a lesson."

Uncle Wiggily thought about it for a long time and then made up a plan, telling no one about it.

"I'll dig a hole at the end of the garden," said the rabbit gentleman to himself, "for it is there that Bunty most often runs to when she runs away. And I'll hide myself in the hole. Then, when Bunty comes along, running away as she is sure to do sooner or later, I'll call 'Boo!' at her.

"When I cry 'Boo!' from the hole where I am hidden this will make Bunty stop and think. And if she stops and thinks she won't run away. It's a good plan, I'm sure."

So Uncle Wiggily dug a deep hole in the soft dirt at the end of his garden, and in the hole he hid himself the next day. There he waited for Baby Bunty to come so he might cry "Boo!" at her.

But the funny part of it is that after he had crawled into the hole Uncle Wiggily fell asleep. He meant to stay awake, but it was so warm and cozy in the hole that he fell asleep.

Soon after Uncle Wiggily had fallen asleep in the hole, Baby Bunty started to run away again. She slipped softly off the front porch and tiptoed down the garden. At the lower end she saw a hole.

"Oh! I wonder what's in the hole?" thought Baby Bunty. "I'll poke a big stick down the hole and find out." So Baby Bunty poked a big stick down in the hole. She poked the stick and she twisted the stick and she jabbed the stick and then, all of a sudden, out of the hole popped the Fuzzy Fox.

"Hi Yi!" yipped the Fox. "What do you mean by poking, jabbing and twisting me with a stick? I hid in the hole to get Uncle Wiggily, and you poked me out, Baby Bunty! Oh, how you poked me right in the ribs! And you jabbed me on my nose!"

"I'm glad I did!" laughed Baby Bunty, and when she shook her big stick at the Fox, away he ran. "Ho! Ho!"

laughed Baby Bunty, and when she laughed Uncle Wiggily, in his hole, awakened. He was in a different hole from the one where the Fox had hidden himself.

"Boo! Boo!" cried the bunny rabbit gentleman, but Bunty only laughed harder and said:

"Pooh! You can't scare me! I wasn't scared of the Fox, so I'm not scared of you, Uncle Wiggily! Ho! Ho!"

And Uncle Wiggily was very much surprised when he heard what had happened while he was asleep. But Baby Bunty was very good—she didn't run away any more that week. And Nurse Jane said the little rabbit girl was very clever to poke and jab the Fox with her stick.

Now if the pussy cat don't try to tickle the goldfish with her tail I'll tell you next about Uncle Wiggily trimming the hedge.

STORY XXVII

UNCLE WIGGILY TRIMS THE HEDGE

Uncle Wiggily and Mr. Whitewash, the good, kind polar bear gentleman, were walking along the woodland path together. Soon they came to the parting of the ways. One path led to the bunny rabbit gentleman's hollow stump bungalow, and the other to the cave of Mr. Whitewash.

"Well, good-bye," said Uncle Wiggily, making a low and polite bow with his tall silk hat to the polar bear gentleman.

"Good-bye," said Mr. Whitewash. "If you haven't anything to do, Uncle Wiggily, come over to see me tomorrow and I'll fry you an icicle pancake."

"Thanks, I'd love to," said Mr. Longears, "but tomorrow I must trim the hedge."

"Trim the hedge—what do you mean?" asked the polar bear.

"I mean I must clip and cut off the long, straggly hedge ends to make it nice and smooth," answered Uncle Wiggily.

"I'll take a big pair of scissors, bigger than any barber pig ever used, and trim the hedge. After I do that I may come over to see you."

"Please do," invited Mr. Whitewash.

Uncle Wiggily hopped one way and the polar bear gentleman shuffled off the other way. And behind the sassafras bush the Fuzzy Fox said to the Woozie Wolf:

"Did you hear that?"

"Did I hear what?" snarled the Woozie Wolf, who was hiding in the sassafras bush with the Fuzzy Fox. They had hoped to catch Uncle Wiggily to nibble his ears. But when they saw the big, strong polar bear gentleman with the rabbit the Fox and Wolf were frightened and kept scrouched down under the sassafras bush.

"Did you hear what Uncle Wiggily said about going to trim his hedge tomorrow?" whispered the Fox to the Wolf.

"Well, what of it. What's a hedge, anyhow?" asked the Wolf.

"A hedge," said the Fox, "is a green fence growing around the hollow stump bungalow. It grows and grows and it needs trimming now and then. Uncle Wiggily will trim his hedge tomorrow and it will be a good time for us to catch him and nibble his ears."

"How?" asked the Wolf, sort of hopeless like and indifferent. "We have tried so many times to nibble that rabbit's ears," he said, "and each time we fail so—what's the use?"

"There will be lots of use this time," declared the Fox. "Early in the morning I will slink around and hide myself in the middle of the thick, green hedge. Then, when Uncle Wiggily comes with his big shears to do the trimming, I'll grab him."

"It sounds all right," whispered the Wolf. "If you catch him I'll help nibble his ears."

"Thank you," said the Fox politely. That is as politely as a Fox ever speaks.

Then the two bad animals slipped away; the Fox to wait until morning, when he would try to catch Uncle Wiggily.

The next day, after breakfast, Mr. Longears took his big hedge shears and started to clip the straggly branches from the growing green fence around his bungalow.

But before this the Fox had softly left his den in the deep, dark, dismal woods and had wiggled and crawled inside the hedge. There he was, hidden from sight, waiting his chance to catch the bunny rabbit gentleman.

And the worst of it was that Uncle Wiggily knew nothing of this. He didn't know the Fox was hiding inside the hedge.

"Clip! Clip!" went Uncle Wiggily using the hedge shears. "Clip! Clip!"

"My, how fast you are working!" called Nurse Jane from the door of the hollow stump bungalow. "You sound like Mr. Twistytail, the barber pig gentleman, cutting Jackie Bow Wow's hair."

"Well, trimming a hedge is like cutting hair," laughed Mr. Longears. "But the reason I am hurrying is because I want to go over to the cave of Mr. Whitewash, the polar bear, and have a fried icicle."

"Well, I wish you luck," said Nurse Jane as she went back into the bungalow.

Uncle Wiggily kept on clipping the hedge and then, all of a sudden, looking down, he saw the big dusting brush tail of the Fuzzy Fox.

"Oh, ho!" thought Uncle Wiggily. "There is the Fox hiding to get me. Well, I see him, but he hasn't got me yet, though he may see me. No, I guess he hasn't seen me, for his back is toward me. Now for a trick on that Fox."

Uncle Wiggily reached over with his big hedge shears, and gently snipped off the tippy top of the tail of the Fox hiding in the hedge.

"Oh, wow! Oh! zowie! Ouchie! Wowchie Zoop!" howled the Fox and he ran out of that hedge and ran home to his den, faster than he had run in to hide.

"Ha! Ha!" laughed the bunny. "I trimmed the hedge and I trimmed the tail of the Fox! I'm a good trimmer!"

And when the Wolf saw the nipped tail of the Fox the Wolf said: "I told you so!"

But the bunny's ears weren't nibbled, and if the rice pudding doesn't hide under the table and pinch one of its legs with a clothes pin, I'll tell you next about Uncle Wiggily and the tree toad.

STORY XXVIII

UNCLE WIGGILY AND THE TREE TOAD

Once upon a time the Woozie Wolf knocked at the door of the den where lived the Fuzzy Fox.

"My goodness!" barked the Fox as he opened the door. "You are getting very polite all of a sudden! What's the idea?"

"I thought perhaps you might have company," growled the Wolf, and then, finding there was no company in the den of the Fox, the Wolf didn't act polite any more. Some folks are like that; aren't they?

"I came over to tell you a new way to catch Uncle Wiggily," growled the Wolf.

"How?" asked the Fox. "We've tried every way I know and none has been of any use."

"This time we'll catch him," went on the Wolf. "I have old Hoo Hoo the owl to help us."

"What good can that owl bird do?" asked the Fox.

"He can see in the dark much better than you and I," spoke the Wolf. "Hoo Hoo the owl is going to perch in a tree near Uncle Wiggily's hollow stump bungalow. Whenever Uncle Wiggily goes out after dark, as he is sure to do sooner or later, Hoo Hoo the owl will fly and tell us. Then we can race through the dark woods and catch that rabbit before he knows it."

"Maybe we can and maybe we can't," whined the Fox. "However, we'll try it."

So Hoo Hoo the owl took his place in a tree outside the hollow stump bungalow.

After a while Uncle Wiggily, who had eaten his supper of broiled carrots with turnip sauce on them, hopped out of his hollow stump bungalow.

"Where are you going!" asked Nurse Jane Fuzzy Wuzzy.

"I am going to look for an adventure!" Uncle Wiggily answered to his muskrat lady housekeeper.

"But it's dark!" squeaked Nurse Jane.

"So much the better for adventures!" laughed the bunny gentleman. "But I will not be long. I am just going to the movies with Uncle Butter, the goat."

As soon as Uncle Wiggily hopped from his hollow stump bungalow, Hoo Hoo the owl saw him. Flying on his soft, fluffy wings, the bird of the night told the Wolf and Fox.

"Ah, now we'll catch that rabbit!" snickered the Wolf.

Uncle Wiggily hopped along through the dark woods. All of a sudden, as he passed under an oak tree, he heard a sad voice saying:

"Oh, I've fallen out! I've fallen out and I can't get back again! Oh dear!"

"My goodness! That can't be a bird who has fallen from its nest!" thought Uncle Wiggily. "For the time of nesting birds is over. I wonder who it is?"

In his pocket Uncle Wiggily had a little flash light made of some lightning bugs corked up in a bottle with honey to eat when they felt hungry. Flashing his lightning bug bottle on the ground, the bunny gentleman saw a little green toad.

"Was that you talking about having fallen out?" asked the bunny. "I didn't know toads had nests from which they could fall."

"I am not a regular toad," was the answer. "I am a tree toad and I live in this oak tree. But I just fell out and hurt my back."

"That is too bad," spoke Uncle Wiggily. "I'll help you." So he put the little greenish gray toad back in a forked crotch of the tree and the toad began to chirp in a happy voice, something like a cricket or grasshopper.

"Thank you, very much, for having helped me," sang the tree toad.

"Oh, don't mention such a little thing as that," answered Uncle Wiggily, shining his firefly flash light on his pink nose to see if it was twinkling properly. And it was.

And just then, led by Hoo Hoo the owl, along came the Fuzzy Fox and the Woozie Wolf through the dark forest.

"Ah ha! Now we have Uncle Wiggily!" growled the Wolf.

"Now we shall nibble his ears!" howled the Fox.

"And you must give me a share for having led you to him!" called Hoo Hoo the owl.

The Fox and Wolf caught Uncle Wiggily by his ears, but before they could nibble him, there was a queer, trilling whistle in the oak tree and then, down showered a lot of hard acorns, hitting the Fox and Wolf on their noses.

"Oh, that must be the police!" howled the Wolf.

"Yes, I guess so," agreed the Fox. "I heard the police whistle and they're throwing bullets at us. Let's run!"

"I'd better fly, too," croaked Hoo Hoo the owl.

So away ran the Fox and Wolf and away the owl bird flew. And then the little tree toad laughed.

"I fooled the bad chaps with my trilling whistle and by throwing acorns at them," he laughed.

"Indeed you did!" chuckled Uncle Wiggily. "Now it is my turn to thank you."

"Oh, don't mention such a little thing," said the tree toad. And with a low and polite bow Uncle Wiggily hopped on to go to the movies with Uncle Butter, having had a wonderful adventure.

And if the hat pin doesn't try to jump through the toy balloon and make it pop like a soda water bottle, I'll tell you next about Uncle Wiggily and the little tent.

STORY XXIX

UNCLE WIGGILY AND THE LITTLE TENT

Splish, splash! Down came the rain in Woodland where the animal boys and girls lived.

"Oh, dear!" sighed Susie Littletail, the rabbit girl. "I can't take my dollie for a ride when it rains, for she'll catch cold in her shoe button eyes."

"Oh, dear!" sighed Billie Wagtail, the goat boy. "When it rains I can't fly my kite, for the water would soak off all the paper."

"Oh, dear!" sighed Kittie Kat, the pussy girl. "Now I can't go to the movies, for my tail will get all wet in the rain."

But Toodle and Noodle Flat Tail, the beaver boys, didn't mind the rain at all, for they loved water. So they swam about, flipping and flopping their broad flat tails.

Pretty soon, as Toodle and Noodle were swimming across the duck pond, they saw, on the far side, Baby Bunty, the little rabbit girl, under a big umbrella, off which the rain drops were splashing.

"Whoo-oo, Toodle! Whoo-oo, Noodle!" called Baby Bunty from the bank of the duck pond.

"What's the matter?" asked Toodle and Noodle, as they swam close to the little rabbit girl.

"I want to go to Uncle Wiggily's hollow stump bungalow," said Bunty, "but it is raining so hard I'm afraid I'll never get there."

"We'll help you," kindly offered Toodle. "We'll put you in a box boat and pull you to the other side of the duck pond, and then you can easily go to Uncle Wiggily's."

Soon the beaver boys found a box for a boat. Baby Bunty sat in it, holding her umbrella over her head to keep off the rain. Toodle and Noodle swam on ahead, pulling the box boat behind them, and soon they were at the other side of the duck pond. From there it wasn't far to the hollow stump bungalow.

"Why, Baby Bunty! However did you get out with all this rain?" asked the bunny gentleman, as he let in the little rabbit girl.

"I came under my umbrella like a little tent," answered Bunty, "and Toodle and Noodle pulled me across the duck pond in a box boat."

"That was kind of them," spoke Uncle Wiggily. "And now you had better go in the kitchen and Nurse Jane will give you a glass of warm milk to keep you from catching cold. And you'd better take off your shoes, for your feet are wet."

Uncle Wiggily went on reading his book, trying to learn new ways of twinkling his pink nose, and pretty soon Baby Bunty, with dry feet, came creeping into the room where the bunny gentleman sat.

"Uncle Wiggily," said Baby Bunty, "I came over to play with you, but you don't play—you just read a book all the while!"

"Ah, bless your little ears!" laughed the rabbit gentleman. "I must play with you a bit, I suppose. What shall we do?"

"Let's make a little tent and have a play party in it," said Bunty.

"How can I make a tent inside my bungalow?" asked Uncle Wiggily.

"Make it out of my umbrella," said Bunty. "Open the umbrella and put it on the floor and we can crawl in it and play party. That will be lots of fun!"

"All right!" laughed the bunny gentleman. So he opened the umbrella, which was nearly dry by this time, and put it on the floor in the dining room near the table.

But when both he and Baby Bunty tried to get inside the little umbrella tent, there wasn't room.

"We must have a bigger tent," said Bunty. "I know how to make it. Take the table cloth, Uncle Wiggily, and put it over the umbrella. That will make a fine tent."

So the rabbit gentleman did this, and with the table cloth on top of the umbrella, and hanging down the sides, the little tent was big enough for both of them.

"But now we must have something to eat for the play party," said Bunty. "I know what you can do, Uncle Wiggily. Please go ask Nurse Jane for some cake—cake is fine for play parties in a little tent. Oh, I'm having a lovely time!" she cried.

"Well," sighed Uncle Wiggily, "I'm glad of that, Bunty." So he went to the kitchen and got some cake from Nurse Jane, and hopped back into the tent with it so Bunty could have a play party. And all of a sudden just as they were eating the cake, all of a sudden there was a popping sound and the table cloth and umbrella tent fell down on the heads of Uncle Wiggily and Baby Bunty.

"Oh, the Fox is after us and so is the Wolf!" cried Bunty.

"Help! Help!" shouted Uncle Wiggily.

"My goodness! What in the world has happened?" gasped Nurse Jane. The muskrat lady housekeeper ran into the dining room. There was no Fox there and no Wolf. Nurse Jane pulled the umbrella and table cloth up off Uncle Wiggily and Baby Bunty.

"What happened?" asked Mr. Longears. "Did the Skillery Scallery Alligator try to nibble my ears?"

"Nonsense!" laughed Nurse Jane. "The umbrella just snapped shut, that's all. I guess you didn't put it up right."

"Ho! Ho! Is that all?" laughed Baby Bunty. "Come on play little tent some more, Uncle Wiggily!" And they did, but this time the umbrella didn't go shut.

So they had lots of fun, and if the rubber boots don't walk off by themselves and go to the movies, I'll tell you next about Uncle Wiggily and the clothes line.

STORY XXX

UNCLE WIGGILY AND THE CLOTHES LINE

"Uncle Wiggily, I am going to do a very funny thing," said Nurse Jane Fuzzy Wuzzy to the rabbit gentleman one morning.

"What are you going to do—sing, dance, or make queer faces?" asked Mr. Longears.

"Pooh! Nonsense! As if I ever did any of those things!" exclaimed the muskrat lady housekeeper. "I mean I am going to wash Saturday."

"Wash Saturday? Do you mean that Saturday has a dirty face, or something like that?" chuckled the rabbit. "I didn't know you could wash one of the days of the week."

"Oh, you are a tease!" sighed Miss Fuzzy Wuzzy. "I mean I am going to wash some clothes on Saturday—that's today."

"That's different!" said Uncle Wiggily. "Why didn't you say so at first? Well, do you want me to go to the store for some soap suds?"

"I wish you'd go off and look for an adventure and not tease me!" begged Nurse Jane. "I am washing on Saturday because I expect company on Monday. And all I ask of you is to string up the clothes line for me."

"I'll do that!" promised Uncle Wiggily.

So the rabbit gentleman went in the laundry where the clothes line was kept neatly coiled up. Taking the line over

214

his paw, Uncle Wiggily started out to the yard with it. Near
the laundry door he saw a bag of clothes pins.

"I'll take these out and leave them on the grass for Nurse
Jane," he said. "I won't tease her any more about washing
the face of the clock or anything like that."

Now it was about this time that the Skillery Scallery Alligator with humps on his tail set out from his den in the
swamp to go out looking for ears to nibble. And the 'Gator
had not gone very far before he met the Bob Cat.

"Where are you going?" asked the Bob Cat of the 'Gator.

"I'm looking for ears to nibble," said the 'Gator.

"Good! So am I," said the Bob Cat. "And I know where
Uncle Wiggily is at this moment."

"Where is he?" asked the 'Gator.

"He's out in the garden, hanging up the clothes," said the
Bob Cat.

"Then I'll come along and nibble off his nose!" sang the
'Gator.

"No! No! Not his nose—his ears!" snarled the Bob Cat.

"Oh, I only said that to make a rhyme like in Mother
Goose," laughed the 'Gator. "You're right, we'll nibble his
ears. But how do you know he is in the garden hanging out
the clothes?"

"I saw him with the clothes line from the top of the hill
as I looked down a while ago," explained the Bob Cat.
"Come on!"

So the Alligator and the Bob Cat went along together.
The Bob Cat wasn't exactly right about Uncle Wiggily hang-

ing out the clothes. He was just putting up the line, but it was near enough.

"Now 'Gator," said the Bob Cat to the hump-tailed chap as they came near the hollow stump bungalow, "you hide down in the far end of Uncle Wiggily's yard and I'll slink around the other end. Between us we shall catch him."

"Very good," whispered the 'Gator, though I call it very bad.

The Alligator hid himself in the tall weeds near one clothes post. The Bob Cat slunk around to get in the front gate. But there was a tangle in the clothes line and it took Uncle Wiggily so long to take the tangle out that the 'Gator got tired of waiting and fell asleep in the tall weeds. And the bunny gentleman, coming up softly to tie one end of the clothes line to the post, saw the bad chap.

"Ah ha!" thought Uncle Wiggily, "the 'Gator hid there to catch me. But he's asleep. I'll wind the clothes line around him and bind him fast to the post."

So, very softly, the bunny wound the line loosely around the 'Gator, intending to pull it tight in a minute and have him fast. But as Uncle Wiggily was getting ready to pull on the loose end of the line into the yard came the Bob Cat.

"Ah ha! Now I have you!" howled the Bob Cat.

"Wait!" cried Uncle Wiggily. "Before you nibble my ears pull on this end of the clothes line."

"All right," agreed the Bob Cat. "I'll help you string the rope and then I'll nibble your ears," for the Bob Cat knew nothing about the cord around the 'Gator. The Bob Cat began to pull very hard on the line. And, of course, the harder he pulled the more he choked the 'Gator. And the 'Gator awakened and howled:

"Wow! Yow! Gazoopie Zow!"

"Oh, my goodness!" shrieked the Bob Cat when he heard this. "The 'Gator's caught in a trap and I'd better run before I'm caught." Then he ran away and when the 'Gator could flounder out of the tangle of line he also ran away, and so they didn't nibble the bunny's ears after all.

And when the line was ready Nurse Jane hung up the clothes and all was well.

So if the piano doesn't try to go to sleep in the doll's carriage and break off a wheel, I'll tell you next about Uncle Wiggily and—

Oh, excuse me if you please!

This book is so filled with stories that there is no room for another. So, if I am to tell you anything more about Uncle Wiggily, and I really wish to, it will need to be in a different volume.

Thus we come to the end, and I must say:

"Good-bye!"

And Uncle Wiggily says:

"Good-bye!"

And I think I also hear you saying:

"Good-bye!"

THE END